MATED IN CHAOS

AN ASPEN PACK NOVEL

CARRIE ANN RYAN

Mated in Chaos

An Aspen Pack Novel

By: Carrie Ann Ryan

© 2022 Carrie Ann Ryan

Hardcover ISBN 978-1-63695-246-8

Cover Art by Sweet N Spicy Designs

PRAISE FOR CARRIE ANN RYAN....

"Count on Carrie Ann Ryan for emotional, sexy, character driven stories that capture your heart!" – Carly Phillips, NY Times bestselling author

"Carrie Ann Ryan's romances are my newest addiction! The emotion in her books captures me from the very beginning. The hope and healing hold me close until the end. These love stories will simply sweep you away." ~ NYT Bestselling Author Deveny Perry

"Carrie Ann Ryan writes the perfect balance of sweet and heat ensuring every story feeds the soul." - Audrey Carlan, #1 New York Times Bestselling Author

"Carrie Ann Ryan never fails to draw readers in with passion, raw sensuality, and characters that pop off the page. Any book by Carrie Ann is an absolute treat." – New York Times Bestselling Author J. Kenner

"Carrie Ann Ryan knows how to pull your heartstrings and make your pulse pound! Her wonderful Redwood Pack series will draw you in and keep you reading long into the night. I can't wait to see what comes next with the new generation, the Talons. Keep them coming, Carrie Ann!" –Lara Adrian, New York Times bestselling author of CRAVE THE NIGHT

"With snarky humor, sizzling love scenes, and brilliant, imaginative worldbuilding, The Dante's Circle series reads as if Carrie Ann Ryan peeked at my personal wish list!" – NYT Bestselling Author, Larissa Ione

"Carrie Ann Ryan writes sexy shifters in a world full of passionate happily-ever-afters." – *New York Times* Bestselling Author Vivian Arend

"Carrie Ann's books are sexy with characters you can't help but love from page one. They are heat and heart blended to perfection." *New York Times* Bestselling Author Jayne Rylon

Carrie Ann Ryan's books are wickedly funny and deliciously hot, with plenty of twists to keep you guessing. They'll keep you up all night!" USA Today Bestselling Author Cari Quinn

"Once again, Carrie Ann Ryan knocks the Dante's Circle series out of the park. The queen of hot, sexy, enthralling paranormal romance, Carrie Ann is an author not to miss!" *New York Times* bestselling Author Marie Harte

DEDICATION

For Grandma Sharon
I miss you.

MATED IN CHAOS

**My wolf hid my fated mates—until the moon
goddess forced our mating.**

As Alpha of the Central Pack, I know we are the
weakest link in the alliance, but I will stop at nothing to
prove our worth and rebuild from our shameful and brutal
past.

Along the way I fell for Adalyn and Nico, but stayed
away, thinking they were fated for each other—and
never me.

When a mating bond is forced on us, our worlds
collide and now we must survive in this new fated life
where rules break and the heat between us boils over.

Only Valac's revenge over losing his mate in our
previous battles take danger to a new level and if I'm not
careful, I'll lose my two mates before I even get a chance to
make them fall for me like I have for them.

And if we're not careful, the darker danger hiding in the shadows might break us all. As Valac's master is waiting. And he's closer than we think.

PROLOGUE

Cole

I HAD BEEN AN ALPHA FOR AROUND AS LONG AS Chase had, and yet for me, it felt as though I was an amateur while Chase fought the vampires in battle after battle.

I looked down at my hands, knowing I needed to be stronger than this. Needed to be better. I was the Alpha of the Central Pack.

It always made me laugh inside when Chase mentioned that he was the cursed Alpha, the one who was trying to clean up after his father's sins.

The Aspens hadn't lost their magic. Hadn't been relegated to nothing. Hadn't lost all forms of bonds and blessings from the moon goddess herself.

No, that had been the Centrals. That had been *my* people.

I stood at the entrance of my small den, knowing that we didn't have the hustle and bustle of the others. We lived and worked outside the den most times because there just wasn't enough space. It was safer for us to blend in with the humans rather than keep all of our people in one place. Or maybe it was because we had blended in before we had become a Pack, and it was harder to leave that practice.

My wolf pawed at me, knowing it wanted to run, to see someone.

But that wasn't an answer.

My wolf wouldn't allow them to be the answer.

I needed to focus on my Pack, the powers that weren't strong enough, and the fact that the Aspens needed us to be at their side. What would happen once they realized that we were not the Pack that they thought we were? We didn't bring anything to the table except our hearts and what little power we had. The Talons and the Redwoods were the ones with all the strength. I felt as if we were failing.

I shook my head and knew I needed to be better. Chase had learned to believe in himself, so damn it, I could too.

Because we weren't a large Pack, it was my turn to be

on patrol. We guarded the small territory between the Redwoods and the Talons on the north side of the neutral zone. And since it was my turn to be on this side of the land, I was nearest to the Redwoods, and our paths crossed more often than not.

So that was why I scented him.

The person that I shouldn't.

It was odd because Nico was nearly my age, but I felt so much older than him. He was the son of the former Healer and a human and a wolf. The son of the Redwood triad, the legendary power base that had brought honor, respect, and hope to the Pack itself.

And there was something special about Nico.

Something that angered my wolf.

Just like someone else angered my wolf.

But an Alpha didn't get to think those thoughts, and I had to remember that.

I turned the corner, knowing that we were probably on patrol together. Nico and Skye often ran together, but I knew she was healing, and now her patrol would be completely different since she was the Aspen Pack Alpha alongside Chase.

I still couldn't believe I hadn't guessed at her powers. Of course, I had never met someone like her before, having only thought it was a bedtime story, not something that could be true.

But there were so many surprises in that family, *in all of us.*

It was a surprise to everyone that I was the Alpha. I shouldn't be. But here I was, and there was no going back now.

"Are you getting all grumpy again?" Nico asked, grinning up at me.

"I'm not grumpy." I growled the words, sounding grumpier. "Shit, I can't help it. I was thinking."

"If that's what you think," Nico said with a laugh. "You in the mood to run?" he asked.

"Honestly, yes."

"Sounds good to me. I would say things have been a little quiet here, but that would be a lie."

"And bad luck," I growled.

Nico just shrugged, and we began our run in silence, since we needed to keep our senses tuned in to the area around us. I was a strong wolf, could shift faster than most, but Nico was fast in general. The magic that he used was a thing of beauty. And sometimes, it took me a lot more than it should to stop staring at him while he moved. I wanted to think it was just admiring his magic, but now my wolf had other ideas.

"Hey there, you guys," another familiar voice said, and we both stopped, Nico nearly tripping over his feet, very unlike him.

Adalyn stood there, a smile on her face as she waved at us, Lily by her side. Adalyn was an Aspen Pack hunter, a beautiful wolf who could fight like nobody else, and Lily was a witch of the Aspens, with barely any power, but used everything she had to protect her people.

They were our friends, but it was odd to see them up here near the Central den.

"Hey there, Addy, Lily. What are you guys doing here?" Nico asked.

Addy? Since when did he call her Addy?

Why was I jealous?

And *who* was I jealous of?

"I'm just escorting Lily here to meet with the Central Healer," Adalyn answered as Lily waved.

"Yes, there are a few things we're going to go over book-wise, and Adalyn wanted to drive." Lily beamed at us, and the four of us stood there, alert since we were still on patrol, but it felt good to be here, to talk to them.

But my wolf was confused.

Just like the rest of us.

"Are you guys on patrol?" Lily asked.

"We are," Nico answered easily. "Do you want us to escort you to the Central den?"

That should have been something I said since I was the Alpha, but I didn't mind Nico speaking since he was better at it, and my tongue seemed to be tied. Something odd was going on, and my wolf and I didn't like it.

"We're good," Adalyn said. "But if I see you on my way back, I'll join you. I'm off for the day, but I could still use a run."

My wolf pushed at me to say something. Anything. "Just keep an eye out. You know why."

There I was, grumpy and growly again.

Adalyn gave me a look Nico seemed to share, and Lily just looked confused.

"Is everything okay?" Adalyn asked.

But I didn't have time to answer. Instead, Adalyn's eyes were wide, and then Nico was growling, and I was throwing myself over the three of them, Lily's scream echoing in my ears.

There was a flash of light, a shrill voice, heat, a burn, and then nothing as a bomb went off in the middle of exactly where we had just been standing.

CHAPTER
ONE

Cole

ALL I WANTED WAS A LARGE CUP OF COFFEE, THE moon shining through my fur, and a place to nap. Maybe not even in that order. But I was the Alpha of the Central Pack. I didn't always get to rest when I wanted to, nor did I get what I wanted.

Maybe I was doing this Alpha thing wrong.

My wolf pushed at me slightly, taking a big stretch. We had been up for most of the night, cuddling a new wolf pup who missed his mother. Kayt, the boy's mom, was out east visiting her old Pack, her own mother having grown ill from a wasting sickness that was rare but not unheard of in Packs. In fact, I had never met anyone with it before, but her mother was ill and needed her daughter and the moon goddess. The infant was too young to travel that far, and she didn't want her baby near that sickness just in case. So, the father, my Pack, and I took care of the pup.

I was grateful that it seemed that Kayt's mother was well on the way to recovery and Kayt would be home the next day.

But that meant a lack of sleep for me.

I rolled my shoulders back, making my way down the street as humans and witches and other paranormals that still hid within their skins walked past. I ignored the twinge, the one that wouldn't go away.

It had been two months since the bomb had nearly killed me. Since I had stood next to three people I cared about and thought I had lost them forever.

Without Nico pulling Lily in the way he had, the young witch would have died instantly. But Nico had covered her body with his, taking the brunt of the impact for her. While I had thrown myself over Adalyn and as much of Nico as he had allowed me to.

I still didn't think it had been enough.

Even with our three respective Healers, each using their magics that connected them to the Pack with their bonds, we were only now finishing our healing. Adalyn had been forced once again into a boot on her foot, the break she had finally healed from the previous battles with the vampires having sliced right open again. Her bones had shattered, her flesh had seared. I could still scent the burn in my nostrils, could hear her scream as we hit the ground.

Nico had ended up with burns over most of his body, a broken elbow, and a shattered pelvis.

While I had ended up with a broken shoulder, jaw, nose, leg, and internal bleeding that had taken Lane, my Healer, a week to take care of.

We were all exhausted from battle after battle with the vampires.

And all of our Packs were injured. Weakening. And I knew we were the weakest.

My shoulder still ached, as did some patches of skin that still felt brand new even after two months. Lane had put in so much of her strength that I was afraid she would have faded if she had kept going.

And it wasn't as if the vampires had stopped attacking us in the interim.

They still wanted to take us out no matter what. That single bomb they had thrown at us from a distance using a drone had only been their first attempt.

Valac wasn't going to back down.

We had killed his mate, and he wanted revenge. Only, he kept evading us.

All of our trackers, the wolves who could scent others' trails from all four Packs, had been able to find the secret lairs the vampires had been using these past years.

All of them had been emptied. From what we had

known, vampires had been made from demons over thirty years ago when the demon Caym had been brought into our world. Through unspeakable tragedy, that demon had taken over the Pack that had summoned him. That Pack had lost part of itself, a sickly and oily substance coating their souls through the bonds that connected them to the moon goddess and their Alpha.

Other demons had come from the hell realm in order to bring him back for punishment.

I didn't know if Caym was still alive.

All I knew was that someone or something had slithered through the opening between dimensions and had been building an army all this time. And we only knew the beginnings of it. The full scope had evaded us, something that angered all four Alphas in this region. Let alone the other Alphas around the world. We were all weary. There had been other sightings, in Texas, in England, with other Packs that were our allies around the world. But Valac and the others had their stronghold in the Pacific Northwest—where we were.

And I blamed myself.

It was hard not to when it wasn't just an unknown Pack that had brought forth the initial demon. It had been the Centrals.

My Pack.

Before I was born, long before I had taken up the mantle of Alpha. It wasn't me who had done this. It had been the other Alpha and his son. They had sacrificed their own Central Pack princess, using her heart and blood in order to summon the demon. And they had committed other unspeakable atrocities. They had killed so many and started this war.

The Centrals had lost our ability to be a Pack. The moon goddess had weakened herself to strip titles and Pack bonds. Those who survived the initial calling of the demon brands had been left without a Pack.

Those elders and submissives that hid the children and weaker ones from the old Alpha and demon.

And those members had children, like my sister and me.

My sister wasn't a Central any longer, having mated into the Talon Pack, our neighbors and allies.

And during that time, the moon goddess had blessed us again. Or at least, some called it a blessing. She had given us Pack bonds to keep us safe, protected. Because a group of wolves not connected by bonds were alone. We had all been so afraid to join other Packs, afraid that we wouldn't even be assimilated or allowed in. So we hadn't had the strength to heal ourselves, to protect ourselves.

And then, from one breath to the next, I had been thrust into the position of Alpha.

And here I stood, the leader of a small Pack with a tiny den, and we're just now trying to get our feet under us.

The vampires weren't making it easy.

"Cole. Are you okay?" I looked over at my Beta, my second in command, and nodded at Douglas. Douglas had been blessed at the same time as I had, an older wolf who had taken care of us as children. Although with wolf genetics, we looked the same age. But for some reason, I always thought that he had a little more crinkle at the corners of his eyes. From a life long-lived. From the protection he had given all of us.

"I'm fine. Sorry, I'm woolgathering."

"I always thought that woolgathering was an odd statement for a wolf."

I rolled my eyes. "Chase and the Aspens are the ones that actually have sheep on their lands."

"True. Although that is a good idea. We have alpacas."

"We have two alpacas. And they don't like us. And I don't think it's because we smell like wolves."

Douglas's lips twitched. "They just don't like you."

"Ouch."

Douglas met my gaze, just for an instant, before lowering it, his wolf happy. I knew he had tried to get me to smile, the weight on my shoulders making that harder than usual.

As the Beta of the Central Pack, his job was to see to the needs of the den itself, to ensure that we were working as a cohesive unit. While our den also had an Heir, Omega, Healer, and others, Douglas had the hard job of ensuring that our Pack was ready for anything that came at them from within, considering that the Centrals were a little different from most Packs.

Case in point, we were helping a Pack member move into their new apartment within the city limits.

The four dens of the major Packs in the Pacific Northwest, part of our alliance, took over the entire territories from Northern Washington all the way down to Northern California. We encompassed the Redwood Forest, the coastlines, Crater Lake, and everything that we could. Our territories also included the major cities that humans, witches, and other paranormals that we were just finding out about lived. That wasn't necessarily meaning that our den was located there. No, we lived within wards within the forests themselves.

At least most of us did. The Talons, Redwoods, and Aspens mostly lived within their own towns within these wards. The Centrals liked to do things a little bit differently.

I figured it was because of how we had started. How we had lived before we became a Pack again. Our original den had been burned to the ground by our own deceit. When the demon was taken back to the hell realm, nothing had been left. Just a scarred patch of land that eventually had grown into a forest of its own, thanks to the blood of all those we had lost.

I knew that I was never going to walk on those lands again without feeling the echoes of wolves past. So we would never live there. Instead, we had a smaller patch of land gifted to us by the moon goddess herself, as well as the Talons and the Redwoods. It was never lost on me that we were able to be who we were because of other Packs. So many of our Packmates lived in the city.

"So, Josiah starts his new job soon?" Douglas asked, and I nodded, box in hand. "Tomorrow he said. But right now, he's dealing with paperwork. Hence why we're moving him in."

Josiah was a newer member of the den, a former lone wolf from the East Coast who had left his den thanks to a growly Alpha who hadn't understood his people. That was always something that I was afraid of, that I would turn into a manic and depressive Alpha who didn't understand who needed him.

So I did my best to be careful, to understand the needs of my people. Just like those Alphas around me.

Like the Aspens, we were recruiting new members. We needed the strength of the bonds to the Alpha and the Pack to keep our wards active. The problem was, we also needed witches and magic. And with the major coven having an issue, something I wasn't even sure I could name, we were losing magic daily. I was always afraid that we were going to be the first Pack to lose its wards, and the protection that came from them. Not only were they protection from outside wolves and forces, but it was also from the humans that wanted too much from us, or didn't want us at all. As in, they didn't want us to exist. And now we had to be careful of the vampires.

Those vampires wanted us dead, they wanted to be

14

the only supernatural powers, so they were taking out their highest predators.

And because they used magic that was far darker than anything we had ever touched, anything we could ever dream, they were winning. Oh yes, we had taken out some of their lairs and kisses, but we hadn't taken out the major players. We didn't know the major demon in charge, and though we had killed Valac's mate, that had only set him off again.

Hence the bomb that had nearly killed Lily and the two people that my wolf wanted more than anything.

But not the man. I couldn't allow the man to want like that. I needed to find my mate when the time came. And an Alpha didn't get two mates. So I knew that the pull might be there, but that didn't mean I could give it any attention.

I pushed those thoughts from my mind and helped Douglas finish unpacking at the house. It was decently easy since Josiah didn't have too many things, but we also wanted to ensure that he had what he needed. So the den maternals had made sure that the fridge was stocked and the pantry wasn't bare—much like they did for many of the apartments that were part of our den structure. We ensured that everyone had a roof over their head. Rent wasn't an issue, we knew how to save and scrape as we had done my entire life. So our Pack would be safe. Even if they had to earn money to protect the den with outside jobs rather than be somewhat self-sufficient like many of the Packs could do within the den wards.

I rubbed my shoulder again, annoyed at the ache. Douglas's eyes narrowed at the gesture, and I waved my hand. "It's fine."

"It's really not fine."

Douglas narrowed his eyes at me again, then shrugged before we both made our way out of the building and back to our cars.

"I'll meet you back at the den? I have a few things to pick up."

"No problem. I've got it."

"You know that Peter won't be too thrilled that you're out here alone."

I barely resisted the urge to roll my eyes. Peter was the Enforcer of our Pack, the one who held special bonds to the moon goddess and the den to ensure safety of both. Meaning he probably didn't want our Alpha out and about on his own.

I let a little bit of growl into my voice, tired and hurting. It might not be Douglas's fault, but I was done. "I'm the Alpha. If I can't take care of myself walking to my car, then we have a far bigger problem."

Douglas didn't say anything, just shook his head and walked back to his car. I probably shouldn't have taken it out on my Beta, but I was tired. Tired that we weren't enough, that our den was split up. Maybe one day it would change, but then again it didn't make much sense to do so.

Our dens were situated the way that they were because for so long we had moved in secret. Now, humans knew we existed. They knew where we lived and most of the magic that we had. They were aware witches and magic were real. Now the coven had to deal with publicity and the stigma that came with who they were, just like we had to when we were first revealed.

And everything had compounded when the vampires had shown themselves to the world. They were working on their own publicity, and I wasn't quite sure what it meant. I didn't know the end game when it came to the vampires.

And that worried me, like most things these days.

"Cole Levin?" an unfamiliar voice asked as I turned, my wolf on edge. I had scented them of course, had known someone was beside me, but they were human, and my wolf hadn't sensed they were a threat. Maybe I was wrong.

"Yes?"

"I'm sorry, you don't know me. But I'm one of the business owners near here."

I nodded. "Nice to meet you."

The woman smiled, though it didn't reach her eyes. She didn't look angry, just tired. I didn't blame her. With everything going on all over the world, a lot of us were tired these days.

"How can I help you?" I asked.

"I just wanted to know if the Packs needed us for

17

anything. Or, honestly, if you guys had any plan for the vampires."

There were a couple of other people behind her, I noticed, and the itch on the back of my neck grew more intense.

"We don't know what their plans are, but we're keeping tabs on them. Doing our best."

I wasn't the Voice of the Wolves. That was Parker, a former Redwood and now Talon Pack member. Thanks to my sister mating into the Pack, we were somehow family. In the distant sense.

"So you don't know what they want?"

I shook my head. "We know what you do." Not quite a lie.

"Oh. Well, that's disappointing."

I sighed, and if she were a wolf, or one of the human or witch members of my Pack, I would have reached out to squeeze her shoulder. But as it was, I was trying to look smaller than I was. To look less menacing. She might say she wanted me for protection right then, but I knew I had to be careful. If I looked like a dangerous brute, like a wolf on edge, I could harm the reputation of my den. This was why Parker was good at this. He could look innocent and caring, yet strong all at the same time. That was not something I was good at.

"Hopefully, we'll be able to find peace. And we can all live in harmony."

"That would be lovely. I just wish I knew what they wanted."

I nodded and was about to say something as a man walked by. "They want us to all rot in hell, just like they should," he spat before he crossed the street, not caring that the woman and the others with her were glaring at him.

My wolf stood on edge, pushing at me to say something. "We want the same as you. We want peace." I found myself saying the words even though I wasn't even sure they were true. Because I didn't know what the humans wanted anymore. They were scared. I didn't blame them. I did not know how we would defeat the vampires, just that we needed to. There was no other choice. And somehow the witches, wolves, other shifters, and humans were going to have to come together to make this happen. But I wasn't the wolf to lead that. My role as Alpha was to protect my den and to work with the other Packs to ensure that it happened. I wasn't the one to bring humans and witches together. I could barely keep my own den together.

The woman met my gaze and nodded and smiled tightly before she left. Her group went with her, and I didn't know if I had helped anything or made it worse.

I didn't have much time to think about it, however, because a familiar scent hit my nose, and I swallowed hard, struggling to keep my wolf in check. It was always so hard to do when it came to him.

Nico Jamenson walked forward, his hair pushed back from his face, a smile lighting up those green eyes of his.

My wolf pushed at me, wanting to nudge him and sniff to ensure that he was okay. That he was healthy. We couldn't though, because Nico wasn't alone. He stood next to another man, the two of them laughing, before he turned to me and stiffened ever so slightly. And then it was as if he put on a mask, as if he wasn't the same man I had saved and who had saved me countless times. Instead, he was just a friend of my Pack. Someone that my wolf didn't want.

Even though that was all a lie.

"Cole. I didn't think you'd be out in the city."

That smooth and smoky voice of Nico's nearly sent me over the edge, and I held in a growl. My wolf preened for attention while scowling at the other man he was with. Because I scented desire on that other man. This human male wanted Nico. And they were on a damn date. I just knew it. And then I couldn't say anything about it, because Nico wasn't mine. I needed to get over it.

Only I knew he was mine. Just like Adalyn was. And that was the problem.

My wolf knew they were my mates. The moon goddess had somehow gifted me with two potential mates.

But I was the Alpha. I didn't get to have two mates.

Meaning that I would have to choose. Something I would never do.

"I was helping a friend move in. I should head back to the den now. Glad to see you are well."

Nico gave me an odd look, and I realized how formal I sounded. I turned before he could introduce me to the man at his side, a man who could be his mate for all I knew. Because the moon goddess was fickle these days. There were potential mates out there for every single wolf. Meaning both members, and sometimes all three in other cases that weren't mine, had to understand and accept the bond. They had to go through the mating ritual in order for them to be mated.

Which meant Nico could sense that I was his, but had rejected me. Because he hadn't moved forward, just as Adalyn hadn't. Instead, my wolf was the one that was screwed up, tormented. I nodded at him and the other man, and kept walking, straight to my car.

I didn't want to see the disappointment or worry in his gaze. I didn't want to imagine the scent of burned flesh again as I remembered him hurting.

As I remembered the fact that Adalyn and Nico had been hurt because I hadn't been strong enough to protect them or notice that a magical bomb of black and spiky dark magic had been thrown towards us.

I had missed it all.

By the time I made it to the area of the Pack dens, instead of going north towards mine, I turned west towards the Aspens. I was meeting with Chase, the Aspen Pack Alpha, and we had training to do. We were the youngest

Alphas in our area, new at our posts, and dealing with the ramifications of our previous Alphas. At least, we were trying.

I waved as I passed the sentries, who nodded at me, lowering their gazes.

With any other den, they may have forced me out of the car so they could scent who I was. But with the way that our Packs were coming up together, our alliance made it so we could go through wards a little bit differently than we could with other dens. I didn't know if other magics could work like this, if other Packs had this. But I knew our four Packs were something special.

The fact that Adalyn was an Aspen, and Nico a Redwood, was a significant part of that.

I pulled onto the main street of their den and got out in front of the daycare center. The fact that Chase had wanted me to meet him in front of where the pups were, the innocents, spoke to me of his trust more than any sentry waving me in would.

I needed to burn off some energy, train a bit, then head back to the den to see what they needed. But first, I needed to get Nico out of my system.

And then another sweet scent hit my nostrils, and my wolf whined.

Fucking whined like a pup.

I turned to see Adalyn talking to a tall man with broad shoulders. Her messy auburn hair whirled in the wind, a smile on her face. Her high cheekbones made her eyes

22

look even more stark and captivating. She looked like she had been training, sweat coating her skin, her sword at her back.

I didn't see a scar on her, nor the boot on her leg anymore.

She looked whole, healed.

And not mine.

She didn't even look towards me. Didn't even register that I was there. Her wolf wasn't running towards me, needing me.

Instead, I was the only one wanting.

Adalyn didn't even turn away. She bumped the man next to her, a man I knew was mated. Cassius, a strong soldier and wolf who protected his own, was Adalyn's training partner. The two laughed with one another, and then walked away, their backs to me, not even registering my existence.

I again found myself alone, knowing I needed to meet Chase, but my wolf whining and drawn to two wolves who never wanted me.

I was an Alpha without a mate, without a bond.

And it was the only place I was ever meant to be.

CHAPTER
TWO

Adalyn

THE HAIRS ON THE BACK OF MY NECK STOOD ON END as my wolf paced, confused, hurt, and angry.

Oh, so angry. No matter what I did these days, the anger that wafted off my wolf seemed to twist around my heart, reminding me that I didn't have a choice in some things. That no matter what I did, holding back wouldn't be enough. That I wasn't enough.

"I can sense your distress. Do you want to talk about it?"

I turned to my friend and sparring partner and shook my head. "I'm fine, Cassius. Are we going to get on with it?"

He raised a single brow, looking elegant and suave as ever. Because that was Cassius. He was one of my best friends, as was his mate, Novah. We had been training together nearly my entire life, having grown up within the Aspen Pack underneath the former Alpha, Blade. When Blade had turned dark, had taken magics he shouldn't have, and had tried to destroy the Pack, Cassius had been there to protect those weaker than himself. He had done things he couldn't take back, just like I had. Our Alpha had forced us into it. Our Alpha had used his power along the bonds to force us to follow his orders. There were some things we had been able to get out of, some things people like Audrey, our Beta and one of my friends, had tried to protect us from.

But Cassius had fallen just like I had. It was his mate that had brought him back to a sense of happiness, a sense of pride in his work and in who he was in the Pack. He was a soldier like I was, neither one of us being blessed with the fortitude and power that came with being part of the hierarchy. He said he was grateful for that. That he hadn't wanted the responsibility of others as he already had for so many years.

I didn't know if I quite believed him, but some part of me had wanted to be more than a soldier. Not that my place in the Pack was horrendous or unworthy. But I wanted to be something more than what I was. And that just reminded me that I was a horrible person for thinking it. I still had the power to protect my friends, my Pack. Why couldn't that be enough?

Cassius pushed at my shoulder, and I pulled myself out of my reverie. "I'm sorry. I'm having a weird morning."

"Then let's get to it. I want to see that new training move that the Redwoods showed you." He held the derision in his tone for the Redwoods, my friends from the other Pack near us, but I knew he was only joking. After years of being near each other but being isolated, we were all finally becoming one large, not Pack, but alliance. We could walk within each other's dens, and while we might be watched and might not be allowed into some areas, we were friends, allies, and had a common enemy.

The vampires.

Valac.

And that was why we were fighting today, training. Because shifting into our other halves, our wolves, cats, and bears took time and energy. And in the heat of the moment, we couldn't only use our claws and fangs. We couldn't use the shifter form that was better at fighting.

We had to be able to fight as human.

Which was what we were doing today.

I met Cassius in the fighting ring, a dirt ring that was used for ceremonial purposes, training techniques, and countless other things.

Around us, there were stone pillars and smaller versions of stadium seats so the den could join here for

Alpha meetings, mating ceremonies, and other events. Today it was just the two of us, as Cassius had wanted to fight in the dirt, and I hadn't minded. It wasn't as if a vampire battle happened in the gym. However, I had fought a vampire outside of a gym in the downtown area because it had slithered itself into the populace. That had been the second time a vampire had been spotted in the city, and it hadn't been the last. There were reasons that the humans were terrified of us, and the vampires. They were scared of anything that they didn't understand, and we were a major part of that. So we would protect them, just like we were protecting ourselves, and how some humans were trying to do the same for us.

Cassius whipped his leg out, and I hit the ground, my head slamming into the dirt, and I growled.

"What was that for?"

"You are daydreaming, scowling, and not thinking about why we are here. We are training. We have to be stronger than anyone else out there. And you're too in your head to care. Now, stop that."

If it was any other male wolf speaking to me like that, I would rake my claws against his face, spit at him, and tell him exactly what I thought.

But this was my best friend. One of the people I trusted more than anyone. He was allowed to talk to me like that. Of course, I was going to kick his ass now.

My claws slid out of my fingertips, a trick that not all wolves could do. It took strength, will, and practice.

Novah, Cassius' mate, was latent and couldn't use her claws that way. There were other submissive and weaker wolves that couldn't do it on command but were training to learn.

My fangs wanted to slide out of my gums, but we weren't biting this session. No, I was just going to use my claws, and I was going to kick some ass.

I swerved to the right as he came at me again before I rolled, getting him in the knee. The action twisted my ankle slightly, and I cursed under my breath.

Cassius gave me a look, studying me.

"That joint still giving you trouble?"

"I'm fine," I spat, going at him again, claw to claw, fist to fist.

Cassius twisted my shoulder, yanking it, and I kneed him in the stomach before twisting out of his hold.

He let out an oof and glared.

"You're putting too much pressure on your other leg. You've broken that leg twice now, back to back. The Healer did what she could, but you need to rest it."

"You're the one who wanted to fight today, so here we are."

He growled at me, and then we were back at it, no longer speaking, just training, using every single ounce of our strength.

One of the last major battles with the vampires had caused me to nearly lose my leg. Wolves didn't get to grow back limbs. At least not as far as I knew. The former

Redwood Enforcer, a man I was slowly becoming a friend to, had lost his leg in a battle with a demon of all things years ago. He used a prosthetic now, and with the new technology, he was faster and stronger than nearly every wolf out there.

My leg had nearly been shattered and then broken again in the bomb that had almost killed the Central Pack Alpha and my friends Nico and Lily.

Cassius's fist hit my cheekbone, and I pulled back slightly just in time, so he didn't snap it.

My friend cursed under his breath. "Stop it. I could have killed you. What the hell is going on with you?"

"I'm fine."

"You're not fine," a familiar voice said, and my wolf stiffened, bristling.

I turned to see my Alpha striding towards me, a glare on his face.

"I said I was fine, Chase."

Beside him, Cole glared at me, and I knew it wasn't *my* Alpha that my wolf was hiding from. No, it was the Alpha next to him.

"If you're not in it, training like that is stupid. You're still healing."

I glared at Cole as he spoke. "You're not my Alpha," I snapped.

"He might not be, but I am. Stop it."

"I'm fine," I whispered before rolling my shoulders back, ignoring the twinge from where Cassius had twisted.

Cassius sighed and shook his head. "I need to see my mate. If you're just fighting to let out anger, I'm not in the mood."

I held back a flinch, my wolf pacing. "I'm sorry, Cassius."

He shook his head. "No, I'm sorry. I knew you weren't in it, and I was fighting full out like we usually do. When you're ready, come back and we can talk. But I figure you probably want to talk to Novah versus me about this."

He had no idea what *this* was, and neither did I, but I let it go as he walked away.

"Do you want to talk about it with me?" Chase asked.

I shook my head. "I'm fine, Alpha."

I lowered my gaze, not meeting his since he was more dominant than me, and my wolf wasn't in the mood to play those types of games. But I did hear the snideness in my tone.

"You make me want to bite the back of your neck and carry you around until you shake out of whatever the hell's going on with you."

I laughed. "You could try. But I'm pretty sure your mate could take you for daring to do that to me."

"I'm pretty sure my mate could kick your ass right now and would enjoy it with the way that you're acting."

"I'm fine." Once again, I bristled, but it had nothing to do with my Alpha. No, it was the quiet one at his side, the one studying me. The one who always seemed to study me.

But that was the problem. I knew exactly why he was doing it. Why he felt that way. And why I would never let him do more.

The moon goddess was playing a tricky game, and I didn't trust her. She might have given me my strength, but I had *earned* it in everything else I had done since.

And then she had tried to give me something else, and I had lost it.

Because I'd had a potential mate before, I had thought I had been blessed by her and the world itself.

I had met the man who would be mine. I had met my mate. My wolf had preened, and I had bowed, and I had loved him. I'd been eighteen and foolish.

Because mates didn't walk away. Yes, the potential was there. That was why it was a potential. You were able to choose your fate once fate gave you the path. But that was the point. Fate and the moon goddess gave you the most perfect person for you. The one that would complete you. The one you could mark as your own and be with and a bond would strengthen who you were and show you a future of peace and happiness.

I had that in front of me when I was eighteen years old.

And he walked away. He hadn't chosen me.

I hadn't been enough for him.

And then he had died in the Aspen Pack betrayal, going to Blade's side, using dark magic.

Leaving me forsaken and alone, not enough.

Never enough.

So the goddess had been wrong. The goddess needed to be wrong. Because my mate would never have been a betrayer. One that had killed pups and friends in order to gain strength.

That would never have been my mate. He may have betrayed me, may have rejected me. But I would have always done the same to him with what he had done.

And a small part of me knew that maybe, if our souls had been linked in that way, maybe he wouldn't have turned the way he had.

But he had never given me the choice. The moon goddess had never given me the choice.

I looked at the Alpha of the Central Pack and felt that familiar tug that told me that the moon goddess was no longer waiting in the wings, no, she wanted to play tricks on me.

Because this man, this Alpha of a Pack that was not mine, was a potential mate for me.

But I wouldn't allow that to happen. I had seen what happened in the past. I'd seen what had happened when the moon goddess chose a mate for me.

So I wasn't going to let her choose for me again.

My wolf stared, confused and yet determined. *We* had made this decision. We would not let the moon goddess dictate our lives. Not again. Not after the mistake that nearly cost our lives and our souls.

"Crap," Chase whispered as he looked down at his

phone. "Riaz is calling. I'll be right back. Don't do something stupid," my Alpha ordered me, and my wolf lowered her head even though I wanted to scream. I wasn't doing anything stupid. I was trying *not* to do something stupid. There was a difference.

"Tell the Alpha of the Starlight Pack I say hi," I said, knowing I would just antagonize the other Alpha in front of me.

Chase looked between Cole and me, then shook his head before he answered the phone, Riaz's low voice echoing on the line. Chase walked away, Cassius having already done so, leaving me alone with Cole.

"If your leg isn't healing well enough, that means that you're putting too much pressure on it as you're training. Wren is one of the best Healers I know. So why aren't you accommodating for that while you're fighting?" Cole asked, and I whirled on him.

"What's your problem?"

Why was I yelling at him? I never used to yell at him. We used to flirt and joke. Cole, Nico, and I were just friends who laughed and fought beside one another. We saved one another's lives. I didn't yell at him and treat him like this. But now I just wanted him to go away. Why couldn't he just go away?

I knew the answer. But I didn't think he did. Otherwise why wouldn't he have said something?

An Alpha needed a mate. They are stronger when they had their mates at their side, fighting with them and helping their bonds with the Pack. The Centrals needed that strength more than anyone. They were the only one of us without a mating at the top tier, since Chase and Skye had recently mated. And they were rebuilding from the ground up. They had been decimated far more than the Aspens had ever been.

Cole needed a mate. But he didn't say a damn thing to me. So was he rejecting me?

Or had the moon goddess been tricky once again and not told him of it?

Because I knew she was being far more devious than I had ever thought possible. Because Cole wasn't the only one my wolf yearned for. And that was another twist of the knife into my soul.

"Come here, I'll show you how you can keep your weight off of your ankle with that one move that I know you like doing."

"I don't need your help, Cole." I didn't sound bitter or angry this time. Just defeated. Too tired for anything. I didn't want this feeling. I didn't want us to be wrong once again. Only, I didn't think I would have a choice. Not when it came to Cole. And that's what broke me more than anything.

That I wasn't going to have a chance.

But I didn't want to make that same mistake, the mistake that had broken me before. So I would do the rejecting, not of Cole, never of Cole. Or of the other.

But of the moon goddess herself.

"I don't know why you are fighting like this, but come on, let me help. You let me help before, Adalyn," he whispered.

"I'm fine."

"Is it because I don't call you Addy like Nico? Of course, he's the only one that I ever hear call you that."

I froze, Nico's name being tossed in between us like that bomb that had nearly killed us. "What are you talking about?"

"I suppose it's nothing." He tilted his head just like his wolf would as he studied me. "Come on. Let's do this." He slid off his shirt, exposing the long, lean lines of his muscles. The ridges of his abdomen beckoned me, and I wanted to lick my tongue up them, just to taste, to feel. His pectorals were hard, perfect for squeezing and kneading.

But I wasn't a cat. I was a wolf. I didn't want this. I couldn't want this.

He smirked as he watched me look at him as if he were a feast for the eyes, and I growled before I sprung. He moved out of the way, so fast. So damn fast. I rolled quickly and back up to my feet.

"How did you do that?"

"Patience. Come on, let me show you."

And then he did. We moved as one—sweaty, hot, with growls and yips. We were wolves in human form, fighting with a synchronicity I didn't think possible.

He was beautiful, a skilled fighter that used more than

the magic of his Alpha-ness to do this. But I didn't understand. Why was this so hard?

Why didn't he see me as I saw him?

But I knew that would just hurt in the end. I didn't want to see him. I couldn't. Not and protect myself again.

Everything hurt, and I was so confused, and I knew that this was only the beginning. So when he slid my leg out from underneath me and I fell, I was ready for the impact of the packed dirt. Only I didn't. Instead, I fell on top of him, him having twisted his body so he took the brunt of the impact. I lay over him, sweat-slick skin to sweat-slick skin, and I growled.

"Why did you do that?"

"I don't want to bruise you, Adalyn. I don't want to hurt you."

There was something in his words, something that spoke to me, but it didn't make any sense. That couldn't be it.

And then the alarm sounded, and we jumped to our feet.

"It's the vampires," Chase shouted. "Come on. They're at the northern gate."

Alert, I ran, Cole by my side. All thoughts of who we could be gone. Because I knew no matter what, no matter how we fought, no matter how I walked away, we would always protect our Packs together.

That was the only promise I could make. The only promise I would keep.

And even as my heart shattered, I knew that though I couldn't protect myself, I could protect my den.

No matter the cost.

THREE

Nico

DARK MAGIC SCENTED THE AIR, AND I LOOKED UP, confused. I usually had a Packmate with me on my patrols, but I was on the outer edge of the four territories, and my brother had needed to return to help his mate. I had taken the last twenty minutes on my own, and therefore when the black magic hit, it hit hard, and I knew I shouldn't have been alone.

I was wolf, I was witch, and the magic within my veins might not release in ways other earth and elemental witches could, but I could move.

So I pressed the magic into the balls of my feet and ran.

The earth itself pushed against my feet, speeding me faster and faster. Far quicker than any other wolf or human or magic user could run.

I could control the earth in ways that kept my speed. It might not make sense to any other wolf, it might make me a pariah in some circles, but I was the one who could use this magic. I couldn't use the magic within my veins to protect other witches and wolves. I couldn't protect my Pack using this power. I could just run. Run and get there faster to help the others. The magic scenting the air was familiar.

Just like that bomb that had nearly killed my friends. Had nearly killed me.

We had survived that attack, but others had not survived theirs.

Between the vampires themselves—blood drinkers and dark magic users who had been formed from demons—and the hybrids, wolves, and shifters that had been turned against their will into a form of vampire that couldn't survive, our Packs were losing.

Not only were we losing people, but we were also losing the power of the people themselves. Meaning humans didn't want us near, and prejudice and violence against shifters were increasing. Hence why my journey today had sent me so far to the edge of the territory. A human encampment had come to try to set up traps for us. They had lost before, back in the wars with the humans that I had lost friends in. And they were doing it again.

But all that didn't matter as much as me getting to where the battle was taking place. I needed to get to the Aspen den, the closest den to where I stood. My friends were there, my people were. And I, a Redwood, was fast enough to get there on time.

I jumped over a log, annoyed that I wasn't in my wolf form. If I had been, I would have been faster. That was how I was strongest, even though as part witch, it seemed like I should have been able to use my witch powers and magical prowess in my human form. And while I could, I was stronger in shifter form. That was the case with genetics.

Because I was the son of the Redwood triad, and I held the genetics of three parents. It might not make sense to any other human out there, but I held magic from not only my witch mother, but my human-turned-magical father and my shifter father. My siblings and I were a contradiction in magic and genetics, and that only made us stronger.

I kept moving and nearly tripped over my feet, my magic stopping in a sudden halt as I looked up.

The humans. Those we had run off before, they had come back. To circle around the dens in order to fight their protest and drop their traps.

Nausea roiled in my gut, and I quickly pulled out my phone, knowing I needed to make it to the battle like my Alpha had told me, but I needed to tell them first.

"Nico, what is it?" Kade growled into the phone. "Did you make it to the Aspens? They need you."

"I'm on my way, but someone needs to come to this location." I rattled off the coordinates, my hands shaking, my wolf prowling.

"What is it? Another vampire kiss? We're on our way."

"Get the Packs or whoever's closer. Those humans? The vampires found them. And it's not pretty."

Tears stung the back of my eyes and I swallowed hard. I might be a soldier, one day possibly becoming a lieutenant for my den. But I was still an emotional mess when it came to battle. I had the strength, but maybe not the inner core that I needed. The wherewithal to deal with the blood and loss.

Because the five humans in front of me had been strung up and ripped into pieces, dark and black jagged magic seeping out of them. There was no blood. There was no blood left. They had been drained.

The vampires were sending a message.

Because they had been the ones to murder near our land, it wasn't enough to do that to any human. They had to be the ones that we had warned off.

And the human government, who only somewhat trusted us, would not like this.

I explained what I saw and took photos, and my uncle, the Alpha of the Redwood Pack, cursed under his breath.

"Nico, there's nothing you can do for them right now. But you can help others. They need you. I'm sending others there, and so are the Talons. But they need your speed. Go, Nico. May the goddess protect their souls."

I hung up, feeling my Alpha send strength through the bonds.

The reason that the Aspen den needed me was because their soldiers were spread around the rest of the territory, training and helping rebuild part of the Talon den that had exploded with another bomb.

We were all pushed to our limits, and I was close enough to help. I was strong, and I needed to remember that.

So I said a prayer to the goddess for the humans that I hadn't been able to save, humans that had wanted to do me harm but still did not deserve what had happened to them.

And I ran.

The scent of dark magic filled my nostrils once again, this time stronger, and I knew I was close. I jumped over a tree that had long since fallen in battle, turning back into earth.

The battle raged in front of me, vampires swarming and scuttling. At least those who were under the control of the stronger vampires.

From what I could tell, newer vampires didn't have as much control as older ones. The longer they had to settle into their strength, the more independent thought they held. At least that's what we had been able to infer. So newer vampires, something that we saw more and more of now as human disappearances increased over the world, weren't able to completely control themselves. They could in small instances, but not all the time. So other vampires, and perhaps even the demons themselves, controlled those weaker.

And those older ones moved with an inherent grace just like the shifters did. And they were on the battle-grounds as well. Perhaps not in the numbers they used to be, but I knew that was only to lull us. Because this was only the beginning. It was always only the beginning.

Wolves versus vampires were on the ground, each of them fighting with all of their strength. They were outside the den wards. The attack must have drawn Chase and the others outside of the protection of those wards. However, with the waning magic over the years and the moon goddess herself having depleted some of her energy from saving us in the past, it made sense that they wouldn't want to try to hide behind the wards. The vampires would just do their best to use their magics to break them down.

I knew that our witches were trying to find ways to stop the power that the vampires held over our wards. Not just them, but the black magic that I scented. Because those shards of jagged-edged darkness could seep into a wolf and bring forth or take back the change itself.

It was a startling and worrying idea for any wolf. To lose control of the wolf was to lose control of yourself and your soul.

I pushed all thoughts of magic and philosophy from my brain, though, because I needed to focus.

Ronin, a newer wolf who had been bitten recently

and was still finding his strength, hit the ground as a vampire under a stronger vampire's command charged. The vampire ripped his claws down Ronin's side. I growled and moved forward, pulling the enemy off of Ronin's prone form. I heaved, tossing the vampire at Cruz's open arms. The Heir to the Aspen Pack grinned viciously and ripped the vampire's head off with one smooth movement.

Cruz gave me a tight nod, and I leaned down, holding out my hand as Ronin slid his into mine.

"Are you okay?" I asked.

Ronin winced and touched his bleeding side. "I'm fine."

"You will be," Wren snapped as the Healer came forward and put her hands over his wound. The other wolf let out a shocked breath as the Healer sent her energy through the bonds.

"It's just a patch job. I'll get to more of it soon. The bleeding should stop, though, for now."

She nodded, then moved over to the next wounded warrior, Hayes, the polar bear and her best friend and Omega.

He didn't say anything, just used his large body to shield her from any oncoming attack. Having the Healer in a battle like this was tough on any Alpha or dominant.

After all, my mother was the former Healer of our Pack. Now my cousin was an additional Healer to the Redwoods, our family and Pack having grown so much we had had a second generation blended into our power structure.

I looked over at Valac again, at the madness in his eyes, and wondered what he was thinking.

We had killed his mate in a large attack right before I had nearly been killed. Sunny had died, and Valac had lost his damn mind. And the way he was shooting out dark magic as if he had a whole well of reserves worried me.

Because if he could throw out this darkness as if it didn't matter how much he had, that meant either he had truly lost it and didn't care, or he had found a way to store enough power that he could take out our dens without a second thought.

And that thought chilled me like no other.

"The humans will soon find out exactly the monsters you are. The animals. You took my Sunny. And now I will take away yours." Valac sent up another shocking arm of magic towards Chase and Skye, and they kept running. I knocked a vampire into the path of the magic, the vampire disintegrating in a flash.

My eyes widened, not comprehending.

"They disintegrate?" Cole asked, and I swallowed hard, looking up at him.

"That's something I hadn't seen before."

The other vampires kept moving, and there wasn't time to talk.

I fought at Cole's side, using each other's momentum

and strength in order to take down the enemy without getting hit by magic ourselves.

I had a feeling that Valac had used an alarming amount of power in that one strike in order to try and take out Skye, and because of that, the vampire had disintegrated.

The thought of what would have happened to my cousin, the Alpha's mate, nearly made me vomit.

She wouldn't have survived that; no one would have.

And the only thing I could have done was push something in the way of that. Something that had once been human.

Had that human had a choice in becoming a vampire? Or had they done this themselves?

Another vampire with full control of his faculties sent out a wave of dark magic, and I shouted, pushing Adalyn to the side. She hit the ground and I fell next to her, letting out a choked scream, the magic having sliced into my arm.

"Are you fucking kidding me? I have it handled. Dear goddess. Medic! We need a Healer here." Adalyn put her hand over the wound, and then moved back, hissing under her breath.

"The jagged shards are still there. Damn it, Nico. Don't get hurt because of me."

"I'm here," Wren declared as she came forward. "I can handle this, at least taking out the magic. Dara taught me. But I'm not your Healer, Nico. I can't fix the wound fully." She winced as she said it, and I knew the more our Packs

47

mixed, the harder it was on the Healers who couldn't cross their magics.

"It's fine."

"It's not fine," Adalyn snapped. "You don't get to sacrifice yourself for me. Nobody does."

"You're not helping, Adalyn," Cole put in.

The two of them glared at each other before staring down at me as I sucked in another breath. Wren and Dara, the harvester death witch who had come to stand at Wren's side, had begun their magic. It pulled out the vampire bile, as I like to think of it, but I was still bleeding.

Wren quickly wrapped my arm with a bandage and nodded tightly.

"Get to your Healer. And damn it, I wish we could go across Pack lines. With as many people that have been mating within these dens, you would think I would be able to."

"Add it to the list of things we're trying," Dara mumbled before she moved again, ducking out of the way of Cruz's glare and stomping off.

I didn't know what that was about, but he looked just as angry as Cole and Adalyn did.

There wasn't a lot of time to think, to wonder exactly what the witch—who had more power in her pinky than I could ever hope for—had done and sacrificed in order to find a way to help all of us.

There weren't enough witches within each of the dens to help us. I knew that; everyone did.

With the major coven dealing with new politics and their own internal wars, I didn't know how we were going to take care of the vampires.

But that was something we were going to have to do soon.

I stood up and swayed a bit, as Adalyn glared.

"Go back to the den. You're out of this battle."

"You aren't my Alpha. You aren't my dominant. You don't get to tell me what to fucking do."

I didn't mean to snap at her, but I was tired of her treating me like a child. We were of equal dominance, something she damn well knew. And yet she lowered me to a place that she felt more comfortable. Because God forbid we feel the pull that we always did.

"Enough. Valac is still here."

We kept moving, and I was grateful that Cole had stopped us. We never used to fight like this. But ever since the bomb? Ever since we had nearly died for each other yet hadn't spoken about it, the three of us couldn't be in a room without screaming at each other.

I had even tried going on another damn blind date for coffee, just to get over them. And the first person I had seen was Cole.

Of course. My wolf wanted them both, needed them both, but I had never heard of a mating between three different Packs, let alone with one of them being an Alpha. And my wolf didn't tell me that we were mates. Therefore, it was just an attraction. Something I needed to get over.

We kept fighting, and as Valac moved towards Skye and Chase again, I kept going, trying to protect those that I could.

Suddenly Valac was gone in a puff of magic that brought down more jagged black shards. Wolves ducked out of the way, protecting those around them.

I looked around, confused.

"What the hell was that? Why did he just go?" I asked.

"It sure as hell felt like a distraction," Adalyn whispered.

I thought of the dead humans along the way and the fact that Valac didn't seem to be truly comprehending what he was doing other than wanting revenge.

I wasn't sure what he was doing, or what needed to be done.

But something was coming, something that might even be outside of the main vampire general that we knew.

We began to clean up the bodies, helping those injured, going over what had just happened. I stood on a battlefield, covered in black magic dust, blood of enemies and friends, and was grateful that nobody other than the vampires had died. All of the shifters, humans, and witches among us had survived. I was still bleeding, Ronin was hurt, but we had all survived. This time.

I looked at Adalyn and Cole, who stood glaring at me. I didn't know what to say. I wasn't going to apologize for saving Adalyn. They were just going to have to get over it.

And I just wanted my friends back.

I opened my mouth to say something, and then it happened.

In a wave of magic and semblance and memory that made no sense, a bond between three snapped into place. It was as if someone had taken my heart and cut it into thirds before weaving it back into this amalgamation of who I once was. A bond ripped through me and into Adalyn, and then again into Cole. I looked at them both and fell to my knees, the other two doing the same. My hands dug into the ground as others shouted towards us, and I wondered what the fuck had just happened.

This was not happening. It did not happen this way.

"What is this?" Adalyn asked, her voice high-pitched. "What is this?"

"No. This can't be happening. We didn't get a choice," Cole muttered.

I ignored the pain that their words caused because it was just now making sense.

We stood up, shaking, as people came around us, asking us questions, all speaking at once even though I didn't hear what they were saying.

I looked across at the two people who I knew inside and out now. Who I could feel along bonds that weren't meant to be. Because these bonds did not just show up. They needed to be cultivated, there needed to be a mark, a mating mark in which the wolves accepted one another. We needed to kiss and to hold each other and have sex and mate in order for us to fully seal that bond.

As I looked at the two people who I felt along my soul, I knew something had changed.

That the moon goddess had made a decision for us.

"Mates. We're mates."

Adalyn shook her head, her eyes wide, and resignation slid over Cole's face. I knew the moon goddess had made a mistake.

I had found my mates; he had forcibly given them to me.

And they'd already rejected me.

Cole

An unfamiliar bond tugged around my soul, slowly encroaching on every essence of who I was, and I swallowed hard, trying to figure out what the hell had just happened.

People were shouting, my own Pack members looking at me in wonder, surprise, and perhaps a touch of horror.

Because the Alpha of their den had just been forced into a mating with not one but two people.

Two people that I trusted more than most people. Two people that I had done my best to avoid for these weeks.

And now it seemed that the moon goddess had other plans for us.

"What just happened?" Adalyn asked, her voice sharp.

Nico looked between us, and there was joy in his eyes for an instant before cautious denial slid right back in.

I didn't know what I was supposed to think, let alone the others. Mating didn't work this way. We all knew that. Yes, some of the rules of mating had changed in the past, but not like this, not to this extent.

"Cole?" A gruff voice.

I looked over at Chase as he stared at me wide-eyed, rubbing his hand over his chest.

"Is she in the Pack? Is she in your Pack?" I repeated, trying to remain calm.

Adalyn looked at Chase, her Alpha, her friend, as her eyes filled with tears.

"I don't feel you, Chase. I don't feel anyone. I don't feel the Aspens."

Nico's knees buckled as he blinked. "My family. I don't feel my family anymore."

I cursed under my breath as Chase came toward us. The Aspen Alpha's wolf jumped into his eyes. "I don't know what the hell just happened, but are they in your Pack? You're the fucking Alpha, Cole. Feel them. Because if their Pack bonds are gone, and they're not with you? Then we have a serious damn problem. Is this the vampires?"

They didn't know. Outside of the three of us, they didn't know that we were mates. They just saw the amalgamation of magic and horror as the three of us stared at each other. Chase and the others connected to the Pack would have noticed Adalyn and Nico leaving their respective Pack structures. But they wouldn't have noticed the mating bond. Not if those actions had happened simultaneously.

And that was a problem.

"It's not the vampires," I whispered.

"How can you know?" Cruz asked, glaring at us.

Dara stood by his side, her dark hair pulled back in a messy bun. She looked at Adalyn, her eyes widening. "Because she is a *Central*. Can't you feel it? The new bonds?"

I turned to her. "How could you tell?" I asked the harvester death witch.

"Because mating is magic, Alpha. Just like the magic of the elements and death. It is life. The moon goddess blessed you with a mating. This has nothing to do with the vampires." She paused. "Or perhaps it has everything to do with them. Perhaps we needed this to happen."

I cursed again and then whirled toward the two people connected to me in such an obscene way it didn't make any sense.

"You are Centrals. I can feel it. Whatever the moon goddess did, and it had to have been her, we're mates, without a choice, without a mark. And in doing so, the Alpha's mates have to be part of that Pack. So, you're no longer Redwood. No longer Aspen."

"Without a choice?" Adalyn spat, her hands shaking. I didn't want to think of this as rejection, that she was just scared and she needed time. But what else was I supposed to think when she took a step back, her hands fisted at her sides?

What else was I supposed to think when Nico looked as if someone had taken his heart from him, as if they had ripped it from his chest cavity, leaving him alone.

"We need to go back to the den. We need to talk about this." I looked over their shoulders, around at the wide and curious eyes.

"We need to talk with just the three of us."

I didn't put my dominance in it. I didn't make it an order. Because would I be able to order my mates?

A single spark of intense joy flooded me before I let it burn to embers. Knowing I needed to focus. Knowing this was only the beginning.

Of what? I didn't know. But I knew it couldn't be good.

"A mating?" Chase asked, flabbergasted. "Oh, holy goddess. I've no idea how the hell that even works."

"But I'm Aspen. I've always been Aspen." Adalyn wiped a tear from her face, as Nico moved forward and took her hand. She didn't pull away, but she did stiffen. At least he was touching her. At least she let him touch her.

And I was on the outside looking in. Something I was damn good at.

"Addy. Come on. Let's figure this out. There has to be

a reason. We don't need everyone else listening in on us, okay?"

Nico gave me a pleading look, and I nodded tightly before pulling my gaze from the two of them. There was nothing for me to do right then. Nothing for me to say that was going to make this better for them. They had lost everything. And all they had gained was a broken Alpha.

"Chase, can you finish the clean up? I need to get the few people I have here, as well as my mates, back to the den."

"Of course. You're not alone in this, Cole." Chase's lips quirked into a small smile. "Congratulations, Alpha. All of you." Chase squeezed Nico's shoulders, then mine, and then went to Adalyn and hugged her close.

My wolf pushed forward, jealousy rearing its ugly head. It didn't matter that I knew that Adalyn didn't want me. That though we were now mated, we had barely touched beyond a few casual glances and brushes. Beyond training and saving each other's lives.

My wolf didn't want this other Alpha near her. And with the way that Nico stiffened and his low growl filled the space, I wasn't the only one affected.

"Shit. I forgot about the mating urge. Well. This is going to be interesting." He looked at all of us, then backed away, hands outstretched.

"Figure it out. We're all here for you."

"Congratulations, Alpha," Dara whispered. Then

looked at the others. "All of you." She pulled Cruz and the others away, and I just shook my head, confused.

"We need to go," I said again, this time putting some of my Alpha wolf into my voice. Nico gave me a look, Adalyn glared, and then the three of us were in my vehicle, not speaking, for the most silent and awkward car ride of my life.

My mates hated me, I knew it. And I had no idea how we were supposed to get out of it.

That's how I found myself standing in my home with Nico and Adalyn, wondering how the hell we were supposed to start this.

"Have I ever been inside your house before?" Nico asked as he looked around, studying my small but tidy home. Most homes of Alphas were a lot larger than mine. Not because we deserved it, but because it was a meeting place, a central place for the den. I could fit most of my Pack on my land, if not within the building itself. It was hard for me when we had first built this den from the ground up to spend those resources and time on my place when others needed it more than I did. Our Healer's clinic and our small daycare were the first buildings I wanted to build. But others had wanted to ensure I had space too. I know it always felt weird wanting more. But then again, I never felt like I was lacking. Now, as I watched two people who had been ripped from their connections to the Packs that they were born into and had bled for, I had to wonder if I was enough.

"It's not much, but it's home. It's the Central den."

Nico gave me a look that I couldn't quite decipher. "Your home is welcoming. Just like any other Alpha. I was just wondering if I had been here before, and I hadn't. I've been on your land countless times. But mostly in the meeting locations or on the perimeter helping with patrol. I just found it odd that I've been to all of the other Alpha homes, thanks to my parents, but never in yours."

I knew Nico was trying to break the tension, and I was grateful for it. I wanted to reach out and pull them both to me. To mark them as mine and finally let the tension sliding through me day in and day out when it came to the two of them slide away.

"Most people don't come here. We're not the center of this alliance, unlike what the title of our Pack may say."

"You're starting from the ground up. And you've come a long way. Don't be ashamed of your Pack." Adalyn cursed. "I'm sorry. I don't know why I'm so angry. Oh, wait, I do. Because this mating was forced on us."

I knew she didn't mean to hurt with her words. No, she was hurting, so I would be calm. Or at least pretend I could be. "I'm not ashamed of my Pack. We're small. Smaller than all of the others. It's harder for people to want to join us. Because while your Pack might have been twisted in some essence, the same with the Talons, the Redwoods were the ones that were decimated by us. We were the ones that brought the demon that started all of this."

There was no use hiding history when Nico's family had lived it before either one of us was born. Adalyn had dealt with her own hells and had even been alive during the first war with the demon.

"I am much older than both of you. I'm a cougar in every sense of the word," she said with a roll of her eyes, and it was good to see some humor back on her face. "I was alive during the last Central Pack war. I met your former Alpha. I met your parents. And then Blade decided to hide all of us and all of our secrets in the Aspen Pack because he didn't want the world to know of his dark magic, about bears and cats, and what kind of witches we had. He wanted to keep all that to himself because he thought somehow he could be more powerful. That is what our history is as Aspens." She paused, a stricken look crossing her face. "Or, how the Aspen Pack was. Because they're not my Pack anymore. I'm a Central, and I don't even know your history. Only what I lived."

"My Pack might be the largest one, might be more settled, but the Redwoods? We had traitors just like you. No one is perfect. But I suppose I'm a Central now. Just how did that happen?"

My wolf preened, yearning for the two in front of us. I wanted these two. I always had, and that was the problem. But I couldn't have them.

I began to pace, pushing my hair back from my face. I needed a haircut; I usually kept it longer on top and shorn at the sides. Even my beard was getting long, getting past that itchy phase that meant it was going to be too coarse for whomever I kissed. I nearly froze, thinking that it wouldn't be anyone else. It would only be these two in front of me.

"I don't know why the moon goddess did this. She's changed matings in the past. Maybe this is something else."

"This isn't mating at first sight," Adalyn said softly.

"No, because we've seen each other long before." Nico looked between us. "And we've all felt that pull. But for some reason, all of us have stepped away. Should we talk about why, or would that be too important right now?"

"Nico," I began, as Adalyn looked up. But Nico shook his head.

"No. Let me talk. Let's figure this out. Or at least let me speak my truths. In the past, it used to be you would sense something along your connection to your wolf, and they would tell you that person was your potential mate. And you would court each other, then mark each other, and then cement the bonds in the ways of human and wolf. That was how it was done. And then mating changed like with my cousin. He couldn't feel his mate because of how the connections had shattered. In others, it took more than just a mere moment. It took weeks or years of being near one another to realize that they were mates. Mating isn't a one-and-done deal. It isn't all or nothing right away. There are choices. I thought, well, maybe one of you could be mine. But then the pull was both ways, and yet not enough. I didn't understand, and neither one of you had ever said anything or moved towards me for anything. So I didn't think I would be in a triad like my parents. And I was wrong. And the moon goddess showed us full tilt exactly how wrong I was. But now what do we do?"

"I didn't want you," I said, surprising myself for even speaking.

Adalyn snorted. "Well, that isn't just the best welcome ever."

"I'm Alpha. Alphas don't get two mates. Don't you understand that?" I slid my hand through my hair again. "I thought you two were mates, and I was on the outside looking in. I didn't want to encroach."

Nico blinked. "And you didn't ask?"

"I could say the same to you." I stood in front of him, looking at him, Adalyn off to the side. I hated this. I had never been in a poly relationship before. The idea of having a triad was never something truly cemented in my mind because of where I stood in the hierarchy. But here I was. With two mates, and I had never even kissed them.

"I can feel you, both of you. Along the bonds. I can sense you. And I don't know how our bond will evolve into who we need to be for each other. But it's there. There's no going back."

"The only people that I know who broke their mating bond nearly killed themselves in doing so, and it was a betrayal that no one ever speaks of," Nico added.

My wolf whined at just the idea of breaking a bond. "I'm an Alpha. I would never break a bond with any Pack member, let alone my mates."

"So it's here. And I don't know what I'm supposed to do from here."

Nico turned and cupped her face. "Then we figure it out." He leaned forward and brushed his lips along hers and I felt the bond shimmer. As if it was just the first cornerstone that brought us together. Adalyn's eyes widened as she pulled away and then looked at me. I did the only thing I could do. I leaned forward and took her lips with mine. She was soft, tasted of the smoke from the battle, and yet all Adalyn. She moaned against me, even as she pulled away, and then pressed her hand to her lips. She looked so innocent, so scared. Even though I knew Adalyn was never scared. Never truly. Because she was the strongest person I knew. And that's when Nico grabbed my chin and brought me down for a kiss. He was only a couple of inches shorter than my 6' 4", so he was tall, broad, and all muscular. His kiss was harder, firmer. As if he was the one leading this. And perhaps he was.

Because I sure as hell didn't know what I was doing.

I backed away, just slightly, as I stared at them both, wondering how my life could be changed so irrevocably and yet feel the same and right all at once.

"So we start here," Nico said. "The goddess gave us each other."

I nodded, knowing he was right. "And we need each

other. So we'll figure the rest out. I don't know what this means for our dens, but we have an alliance. We will always be there for each other. All four of the Packs. But we're together now. Somehow."

Adalyn just shook her head, and my wolf whined, disappointment slamming into me.

"What? Do you not want this? Do you want to try to break the bond?" I asked softly, even though I was breaking inside. "I'll find a way if you need to. I'll never force anything on you."

Nico was the one who let out a whining sound as if his wolf couldn't hold it back, and he swallowed hard. "Of course. Anything you want, Adalyn."

Adalyn shook her head and wiped away tears. "I'm not a crier. I hate this." Then she met our gazes. "I almost had a mate once."

Her throwing a vampire bomb in between us again wouldn't have been as shocking.

"What?" Nico and I asked at the same time.

She let out a hollow laugh. "I was eighteen. And he left me. He rejected me, just like you think that I'm doing to you. And I'm not rejecting you. I just don't know what I'm doing. He decided I wasn't good enough, and then he broke down within the Pack, and I watched him die after he killed my friends. That was who the moon goddess had chosen for me." She shook her head, and I wanted to reach out, but I knew if I did she would stop speaking. Because Adalyn needed to be strong, and though I knew her, the three of us didn't know each other well enough yet for her to break down in front of me. To lean on me. And that would have to change. Now that she was my mate.

I had to stop thinking about that though, about the pleasure that came from that, because she wasn't ready, and honestly, I didn't think I was either.

"I wasn't given a title all this time within the Aspens. I thought I would have been a good Enforcer. Or anything to help my Pack. I had the strength and the dominance, but I didn't think the moon goddess trusted me because of who she had given me before and how I wasn't good enough then. So I never had a title. And I was always trying to get stronger. But it was never enough. And now she's done this, and I'm so confused."

I cursed again, an irate jealousy wrapping around the anger for what that wolf had done to her. "You're the Alpha's mate now. Both of you. You're both Alphas in the way of bonds. You didn't have a title before because this is where you should be. Both of you. So now we figure it out. Together."

And I hoped to hell the words I was saying weren't lies. This changed everything.

CHAPTER

FIVE

Adalyn

I COULDN'T BREATHE. MY WOLF PUSHED AT ME, confused, aching. This didn't make any sense to me. How had I ended up in this position, where I stood between two men who I knew were mine, but I knew couldn't be mine?

"An Alpha's mate? An Alpha? How does that happen? It doesn't make any sense. The moon goddess just doesn't decide."

Nico looked at me as if I'd kicked him, and I hated myself. It wasn't his fault that I was scared. I was scared of what could happen. Of what we could lose. That was all on me. My own fears.

"We don't know how or why, but we do know it's

something," Nico said slowly, as if he were calming a feral beast. And honestly, that wasn't quite that far off. My wolf felt as if it was bucking at the reins, confused and hurt all at once. She wanted her mates, but I was afraid it wasn't going to happen. That it couldn't happen.

I had been given this gift once before, and it had been taken away from me. Brutally, painfully. And now twice over? With men that I respected and liked?

When and if the moon goddess decided to change her mind and ruin it all, I was never going to be able to breathe again. I wouldn't survive the brokenness. This lost feeling that seemed to engulf me.

"Hell, let's walk around the den," Cole blurted, and I blinked, looking at him.

To me, the Alpha of the Central Pack always looked well put together, as if he knew what he was doing, even if he was quiet about it. Part of me had always trusted him to do what he needed to. To be who he needed to be. And here I was, mated to him. I couldn't deny the kiss, couldn't deny the feeling that had washed over me when I pressed my lips to his and Nico's. I knew that bond was there. And I knew there was no backing away from it. Mating bonds didn't break unless you were dead. That was it. The only other time I had seen a mating bond break, or at least heard of one, it had nearly killed all those involved. This was it.

And the harsh realization of what it meant started to come over me.

Because Cole wasn't just talking about taking a walk through the den.

He was talking about taking a walk through my new home.

I staggered back, my eyes wide, and Cole cursed under his breath.

"Adalyn. I'm so sorry."

I shook my head, raised my chin, and refused to cry. "Don't be sorry. If you're sorry, then I feel as if I'm hurting your Pack."

Nico whispered under his breath, "Our Pack."

I nodded, that tug of pain and hope twisting into one. "You're right. I guess we don't get to go back. Even if it doesn't make any sense. But I feel this bond, and that means it has to be for a reason. And I know that I'm going in a thousand different directions, and I'm not being kind, but I need to focus."

"Then let's go see the den," Cole put in, slowly. "Meet the Pack that is now yours. Which is fucking weird to say," he added, pushing his hand through his hair.

My gaze went straight to his biceps, the way that his arms worked as he moved. I swallowed hard, the mating urge brutal at full force. I wanted him. I had always wanted him, and that had been the problem. And now he could be mine. He was mine. And I didn't know what to do about it.

I didn't know if there was anything to do about it.

"So how does this work? Do we just move in and call it

home? Because I'm starting to freak out here," Nico added, for the first time sounding as if the stress was getting to him. And he was the steady one among us. At least when it came to change. Cole got growly, I got my back up, and Nico rolled with it.

Then again, I wasn't sure how we could roll with this.

"Whatever you want," Cole put in. "But hell, what was the goddess thinking?"

I felt as if I had been slapped, and I looked up at him. And he cursed under his breath again.

"I meant taking our *choice*. Nothing else. I want this." His eyes widened as if he hadn't meant to say it. "I had wanted this. Or at least something like it. I already told you I felt that pull. That connection. It isn't going away. If anything, it's getting stronger."

I nodded, my wolf pushing at me. The mating urge rode us in waves, needing to complete the bond. Because while the bond was there, we still needed to mark each other, to have each other in ways that were only just us. But I didn't know how to jump into that. I wasn't sure how to jump into anything at this moment. So instead, I nodded and followed Cole outside.

"Here we go," Nico whispered under his breath before he tangled his fingers in mine. I squeezed his hand, then let go, unsure what to do. Because that touch was almost too much, the sensation pulling me towards him a raging inferno. He let out a short growl as Cole looked between us and nodded, swallowing hard.

Oh, we were all three in that mating urge, and there was no pulling away from it. I wanted to rip off their clothes, lick every inch of them, and claim them as mine. And I didn't think the anger came from not wanting them. No, it came from the fact that I wanted them so much I could barely breathe. But I hadn't let myself think I could have that. So what was I supposed to do now?

"Cole?" a woman with ruby-red hair said as she came towards us. My wolf bucked at the reins, wanting to slash at this woman for daring to come near him. How dare she be in our presence when Cole was mine.

I blinked at the ferocity of that, wondering where the hell that jealousy came from. Yes, I could feel jealousy, but damn it, it wasn't like this. This was ridiculous.

And I knew Jacqueline. She was the Heir of the Central Pack. Meaning she was next in line when Cole stepped down. That was the *only* way it was going to happen. I didn't want to even think about the other option that would lead to her being Alpha. And with the war we were in, it wasn't unheard of. But dammit, I wasn't going to allow myself to think about that. Not if I wanted to survive.

"Jacqueline. You know Nico and Adalyn."

She nodded but didn't raise her gaze towards us. And it was at that moment that I really got it.

I was the Alpha's mate—at least one of them. Meaning I was one of the highest ranked wolves in this den. It was the smallest den of the Pacific Northwest Alliance, so there weren't that many wolves to fight for dominance, but it didn't matter. I was at a level with Cole. While the strength of my wolf wouldn't change, at least I didn't think so, my rank did. And that meant she couldn't meet my gaze. And it wasn't a sign of being better or being cruel. It was just how our animal natures worked. That dichotomy between animal and human was what made us shifters. What made us *magic*.

How would I even blend in with the Centrals? Would they look at me differently? Would they see who I had always been or see the pain in our past connected with the future that we could never get away from?

"The others are here. They're confused. Is it true?" She let out a hollow breath. "What am I saying? I can feel you along the bonds. Of course, it's true."

She held out her hand to me. "Welcome, Alpha. The Centrals are pleased to have you as their Alpha's mate." I swallowed hard and slid my hand into hers. The power was there, the force, and I knew Jacqueline was dominant as hell, just not as dominant as me. It was odd to think that I could feel her along the bonds. And not in the way that I had been able to before with my former Pack.

All people within a Pack could feel each other somewhat. We could inherently scent and sense who our Pack members were. The humans and witches of our den could do the same, so the magic of the Pack bonds made that possible. But now, in addition to those Pack bonds that made me Central, which was weird as hell to think about,

I also had another layer of connection. One that claimed me as Alpha's mate. And I had no idea what I was supposed to do with that.

"Jacqueline. It's good to see you again." I let my hand fall as she held her hand out to Nico. Nico grinned and gripped her hand tightly.

"I guess when we fight in our training, things are going to get interesting," he said, trying to lighten the mood. I smiled. I couldn't help it. Because that was Nico, always trying to make things better for those around him. He would do great as an Alpha's mate. Not quite the leader in charge, not quite the one who held the mantle and needed to be the strength of that Pack, but the one who could be by the Alpha's side. Who would readily be an ear for the Alpha to aid in whatever was needed.

I never thought that would be me. And I wasn't quite sure I would be good at it. After all, I hadn't thought I would ever mate, not after the disaster that was my first potential.

"Going to be interesting for sure. I know you three probably need some time alone," she said, as her cheeks reddened ever so slightly.

Oh, she could scent the mating urge on us as well, but I was doing my best to ignore it, even if it wasn't easy.

"The rest of the den is either on their way here or still at work."

Cole nodded. "It was a surprise for all of us."

"And I don't want to mess things up," I added, not meaning to say anything at all.

Cole looked at me, then turned to face me completely, pushing my hair away from my face. I wanted to lean into him, to let myself submit for just an instant, and I wondered where that came from. That wasn't me.

"You won't. It's okay, Adalyn. We're all just as confused."

Jacqueline cleared her throat. "I think the three of you should go back into that house and figure something out. The aggression between the three of you? Is even pushing at me, and I'm mated." Jacqueline grinned, and I swallowed hard.

"Oh."

"Well, that's going to rub off on the adolescent males a little too much, isn't it?" Nico asked, then cringed. "I probably should have thought of better wording for that."

I couldn't help it, I threw my head back and laughed, the tension easing slightly, though not enough.

"We're going to have a Pack meeting in order to introduce them, but you're right, we need to go back in. To think. And I need to talk with the other Alphas." Cole ran his hands over his hair again, and I wanted to reach out and fix it. It was just a small motion, my hands flicking to do so, before I froze, realizing that I didn't know how to touch him, what we were supposed to do. I didn't know my place, and as someone who had been so strong in knowing that, even if I hadn't particularly liked where I had been, it was odd.

Nico saw the motion and ran his hand down my arm before nudging Cole. "Come on, let's head out and figure out exactly what we're supposed to be doing."

"That doesn't sound very helpful," Cole grumbled, and I grinned.

"Okay. I guess we'll see you later, Jacqueline."

She winked at me, and I blushed. *Me.* I didn't blush. But apparently, the thought that the three of us couldn't even be outside without our mating urge putting everybody into a wild frenzy seemed to send me over the edge.

I followed Cole and Nico back into the house.

My body ached and I swallowed hard.

"Before anything happens, I need you to know, I need to protect this den. That's my role. But the Aspens? I can't leave them behind."

I knew that even as I said the words, they might have been the wrong thing. I was supposed to be loyal to my Pack. But what if I was loyal to the wrong one? While I didn't know what choice I would've made if I'd been given that choice, there needed to be a middle ground. There needed to be something that didn't make me feel like I was breaking.

"Of course, we're going to protect the Aspens," Cole growled. "That's where all of the attacks have been recently. We are in an alliance. You're not leaving your family. You're just gaining more. I know this is unconventional. I know that somehow you're going to have to find a way to think of yourself as a Central wolf, but Adalyn? I spent the first years of my life not having a Pack at all. I know what it feels like to be so confused you're lost."

"I still feel the tug towards the Redwoods, but I feel it in the Centrals as well. We'll find a balance. We're not going to leave them behind. Not when we're still in the middle of a war."

I rubbed my hands over my face, feeling woozy. "I feel like I am unmoored. And I hate it. And why am I having such a hard time focusing?" I ran my hands over my chest, and Cole cursed.

"The mating bond isn't complete," he whispered.

Nico's eyes widened. "So the bond is trying to connect us all by tugging on us."

My eyes met his. "Meaning it's tugging on our actual life force rather than the Pack itself? Fuck. I didn't think it was supposed to happen this way."

"Nothing that we are doing is going how it's supposed to," Cole said with a laugh. He blinked. "Does this mean that we're going to actually have to fuck each other right now to save each other's lives? Because we've hit a new territory that's scaring even me. And I'm the damn Alpha."

I met his gaze and burst out laughing. "Well, that's a line that I wasn't prepared for."

He smiled then, as did Nico, the two of them looking so damn handsome that I could barely breathe. "It's hard to think with you two around. It always has been. But I've done my best not to think about it. Because I didn't think you were mine." Then Nico was there, pushing my hair from my face. It was always such a mess that I tended to do it myself often. But both of them in these last moments had done it, like it was our thing. We were finding our moments, our touches, and I wasn't sure how to even focus on that.

"I realize that this is a little dramatic, but I need you. And I don't know what's going to happen next, but I know there's no going back. And thinking about the past is only going to hurt more." I staggered, the energy pulling at me hard. I hated that these two strong men weren't moving, that they weren't feeling the effects that I was. But then they were there, both holding me. Nico wrapped himself around my back, holding me close, as Cole came from the front, and then I was surrounded by both of them, their scents intoxicating as I tried to breathe.

The world was burning around us, as I knew that the vampire horde would attack us soon, that we would have to find a balance between the four Packs and figure out exactly who we were and how this would work. But I couldn't think about any of that right then.

It was only these two men and the mating urge between us.

Shifters were sexual creatures. We needed touch. We needed taste. We needed all of these to survive. When a forced mating like this happened, apparently, it put all of that into overdrive, and I needed them.

So I tilted my neck to the side, baring myself to them, and Cole let out a deep growl, Nico following.

And when my new Alpha slid his lips over my neck, my knees went weak, and it was only Nico's arm around my waist, the other hand firmly on my hip, that kept me steady.

"I don't submit to anyone. But I need you both."

And there I was, bare, emotionally, if not physically. Yet.

"I don't think I can go slow," Nico whispered, and I grinned.

"Same here."

"Thank the goddess." Then Cole's mouth was on mine, and Nico was pulling us closer.

I couldn't breathe, couldn't think, sandwiched between these two men.

I was tall, at least compared to my friends, but these men? They made me feel small, cherished.

I wasn't sure how to feel about that, and I knew I would have time later. For now, all I could do was breathe between the two of them, rocking myself along Nico's hard cock pressed against my ass and Cole's pressed against my stomach. They were hard, waiting, and I was already wet. The scents of our arousals filled the air, pushing my wolf even further. She whimpered, and so did I. So when Nico turned me to the side slightly, I took his mouth in a greedy kiss, biting his lip as I pulled away. And then Nico and Cole were kissing, both of them rougher, needier. We stood in Cole's living room, in a den that was now my own, in a world that I knew had forever changed, and all I wanted was these two men.

Cole slid his hands up my shirt, then Nico pulled it over my head in one quick moment. I let out a laugh as Cole kissed me hard and Nico undid my bra. Somehow Nico moved around, tugging Cole's shirt off before removing his own.

For a man who was the fastest wolf I knew, it seemed he was living up to his reputation here, making sure Cole and I were keeping up.

When my bra fell to the ground, my breasts were heavy, my nipples pebbled. When Nico moved again, he was in front of me, leaning down to suck one nipple into his mouth. Then Cole mirrored the action, and I was groaning, my knees once again going weak. They both sucked and licked, and I nearly came right there, shuddering at the sensation of both of them laving me with so much attention. They bit down and I shuddered, pressing my thighs together.

"I need to touch you," I whispered, and then Nico was up, kissing me, as Cole undid his belt and slid himself out of his boxer briefs.

I swallowed hard, looking down at Cole's thick cock in his hand, his strokes nearly sending me. That's when I noticed the barbell at the tip, and I blinked.

"I've seen you naked before we shifted. How have I never noticed that?"

Cole grinned. "Probably because I'm trying not to have a fucking erection when I'm around my Pack. It's kind of hard to do, though, when the two of you are naked around me."

"Because we're all trying not to notice that we're naked. And it's usually not a problem. But it's always been a problem when I look at the two of you." And then Nico leaned forward and gripped Cole's cock as well. He bent down, licking our Alpha's dick, and I let out a breath.

"Okay, that might have been the hottest thing I've ever seen."

"We can go hotter," Cole whispered, and then he was undoing my jeans, even as he groaned, sliding into Nico's mouth. Suddenly the three of us were naked, and I didn't even know how it happened. I couldn't breathe with Cole's hands sliding between my wet folds.

There were so many sensations and tastes that I couldn't focus, couldn't do anything.

But I needed to. I needed to breathe.

So when Nico found himself on the floor, his cock straight up as I stroked him, I grinned, kissing Cole again.

"We need to complete the mating bond. That means marks and everything."

"That means I need to feel you," Nico whispered.

I shuddered, knowing that with the urge on us, there wasn't a lot of time. If I wasn't careful, I was going to come right there. So with Cole watching us, I slowly slid over Nico's cock, shuddering in relief. He was big, wide, stretching me. Nico groaned, but then he didn't have time to do much because then Cole was leaning in front of Nico. Nico took that as an invitation, swallowing Cole's cock whole as he lay down on the ground. I hovered over Nico's waist, riding him slowly as I kissed Cole, and our Alpha slowly fucked Nico's mouth. We moved as one, the three of us arching into one another. And then I was orgasming, coming around Nico's cock. I couldn't breathe. I suddenly found myself on my back, Cole licking at my nipples right after Nico slid out of me. I wrapped my legs around Cole's waist, letting my Alpha inside of me, the mating bond slowly wrapping around all of us. It had been a heavy click, a snap into place while on the battlefield. But now, it was as if we were weaving new braids and new strengths within our bonds. I let Cole take me, arching myself into him. And then Cole let out a shuddering breath as I looked around him and grinned.

Nico tossed the bottle of lube to the ground, and I knew exactly what he was doing.

"Goddess," Cole growled, and Nico just grinned.

"You might be Alpha, but it's my turn first." And then we were three moving as one, Cole between us, our Alpha being taken care of in every way possible. I knew that the two of them were decently equally dominant. I knew that they would take turns just as they took turns with me. But I couldn't focus on any of that. Because Nico was moving, and with each thrust, Cole was going deeper and deeper inside of me. I needed them both. My fangs slid out of my gums and I knew what had to happen next. Somehow the three of us were combined, entwined with one another, and I slid my fangs into Cole's neck, marking him as mine. The mating bond warmed, and I could feel these two wrapped around my soul. An ever-present notion that this was my future. Even if I hadn't asked for it, I wasn't going to walk away.

They were mine.

And now I needed to figure out exactly how it felt.

Because I did not love them. Not yet. But I knew that I could. This was a promise. A mating in reverse meant I couldn't reject them, but I couldn't take them as mine yet. And it hurt to think, but they were mine. Even if they weren't at the same time. I marked Nico as well, as the two of them rode each other and me. I wasn't sure who was who or who was touching me. But my wolf knew. She always knew. So after the two men marked me, we three lay in a heap, coming again, finalizing our mating bond in the warmest way possible.

I was the Alpha's mate, marked and bonded and bound.

I had two men who would always be mine, even if I didn't know how they felt about me. And I didn't know what that would mean or how we would change this. But there was no going back.

Because we were at war, and the moon goddess had

needed us to be mated for some reason. So I would face it head on.

Even if some part of me, a small part of me, even as these two men held me close and continued to kiss me and touch me, was afraid that they would walk away.

Because I had been left before, rejected.

And I was so afraid that the moon goddess would take this away again.

Or they would do it themselves.

CHAPTER
SIX

Nico

I swear I could still feel their fangs in my neck and my hands tingled, the earth magic within my veins simmering to the surface.

My dad, Reed, gave me a look, and I just grinned.

"I'm a newly mated male. Sue me."

Reed rolled his eyes and shook his head. "I get it. Believe me. I get it. As do your mom and dad."

For some reason, even though I had two dads and a mother, calling them both dad sometimes had never confused me. Josh and Reed were my fathers, just like Hannah was my mother. I inherited my wolf from Reed, my strength from Josh, and my magic from Hannah. Not all of my siblings had that. It was odd that I had all three of the magics from my family while some of my siblings only had one or two. All of us could shift. We had that much. But not all of us had the magic that I held or the tracking I had a bare whiff of.

My sister Kaylee was the Tracker of the Redwood Pack and held that position because of our father, Josh.

Conner's strength came from Reed with some of the darkness that came from our dad Josh's past.

I also had four younger siblings—because the Redwood Pack triad hadn't seemed to stop wanting to make babies. But I was the only one with my unique talents, and I was still trying to figure them out.

"You're lost in your head again, son. Do you want to talk about it?"

I shook my head. "Not really. It's weird that I'm packing a bag to prepare to move into a house with my mate, and I don't even know the man."

"You know him enough. You've been friends for ages. You know Cole, Nico."

My mother walked in at that moment, her long curly dark hair in a braid over her shoulder. "Your mating came about a little different, but so did ours. And look at us now. We're doing okay for ourselves." She smiled at my dad, both of them looking as if they were the only two people in the world. At least at that moment. I knew if my dad Josh was in the room, it would just be the three of them. They loved each other even more now than they had during the first wars with the demons, when they had come together in pain and agony and joy all wrapped into one.

I wasn't sure how I would be able to fit in the way that I needed to. They blended so well, as if they were made for each other.

And while I knew the moon goddess had a purpose for the way that I had found Cole and Adalyn, it felt weird. Like I wasn't right yet.

"The rest of your siblings are holding off from bothering you and asking you a hundred questions for now." I smiled at my mom, knowing what she was thinking.

"Because they're going to freak out and babble on and I'm never going to be able to leave here with my backpack of clothes? Because of course, I'm bringing a single backpack to my mate's house. Not even my boyfriend and girlfriend. No, I completely skipped those parts."

"You don't date your mate before things happen. Your fathers were never my boyfriends," Mom put in.

"But shouldn't we have? Wouldn't it be less weird if we went the human route and had gotten to know each other before bonds were placed within us?"

"Maybe. But these two were meant for you. We have to trust in fate these days when the world seems to go dark around us. It might be mating into chaos, but you can find your way out of it," Dad added.

I swallowed hard and looked around my room. I lived in the dorms with the other soldiers, not with my parents. I had moved out around the time that my older siblings had, the twins having needed their own space. My four younger siblings each had their own room now, and though they were adults, they still lived with our parents because why not? We lived for eons if we could make it. Our elders were in their hundreds. If we could spend more time with our families, we would. But I had wanted to live with the soldiers, to find out who I could be within the Redwoods.

I looked down at my hands, the magics thrumming within them.

"The Centrals don't have many witches. And the power they do have isn't of earth." I looked at my mom, the strongest earth witch I knew. She nodded as if knowing what I was thinking. "The Centrals need you. So do Cole and Adalyn. I know that girl can fight like no other and can lead. But she's so strong I'm afraid she's going to break because she doesn't lean. So be that pillar. They both will need you, my child." My mom moved forward and cupped my face. And just like that, I was a pup again. I leaned down, my forehead pressing against hers. Both of my dads were there then, standing in the doorway as they watched. They gripped hands, holding each other as they looked at my mother comforting me.

I had grown up with poly parents, in the ménage and triad of legend.

And now I was in the first known triad of Alphas. I was born in legacy, and now it seemed I would be making one of my own.

And if that wasn't daunting, I wasn't sure what was.

"I'll make sure Cole knows that he has someone to lean on. I think he'll let me. We've been friends. Thank you for reminding me."

"And Adalyn?" Mom asked.

"Getting her to do something other than play-fight with me has been the bane of my existence for as long as I have known her. She annoys me to no end, Mom. But I've always had that pull towards her. The same with Cole."

"Then why didn't you do anything about it?" Josh asked.

I looked at my father then, the man who had been human, and now was his own form of magic.

"Because I thought they were for each other. And it never once occurred to me that it could be more. But it seems the moon goddess had other plans."

My mother smiled at me, then patted my cheek. "She always does. Even if we're trying to figure that out. The Centrals need you. As do we."

"You're still a Redwood. Even if your bonds are to others," Reed added.

I swallowed hard. That odd feeling of being displaced fell on me again. I didn't want to be in a new Pack. But saying so felt as if it were a betrayal to everything Cole had fought for his entire life. And I knew Adalyn was fighting it even stronger. While I had a large family to come back to, I knew that no matter what, they would understand. Their own families had blended within the Packs. Even my cousins were members of both Redwood and Talon because of the way the moon goddess's bonds were working.

The Alphas needed to be of one Pack, even if we still had ties to the others. The Centrals needed us. So did the Aspens. They were on the front lines of this war, and Adalyn couldn't leave, so therefore I wouldn't either. I would fight by her side.

Now I just needed to make sure she understood that.

I was mated to strangers that I felt a pull towards, but I didn't love them.

And that made me feel like a betrayer. That I didn't love my mates. I didn't know them yet. I could feel them in my soul—didn't that count for something?

Once again, I pushed my thoughts from my head, knowing that they were too complicated to unravel right then. I had a single bag to sleep over at Cole's house, no, *my* house for the evening. I didn't know what we would do for the future. Cole's house was not big enough for three people. But maybe we'd find a way. I knew that some of the den was uninhabited, as many of the Pack members lived in the city, working there to provide for their people. It was such a different situation than what I had grown up in, and I was going to have to learn the rules.

I said my goodbyes to my parents, knowing I would see them soon. It wasn't like I was leaving forever, or even going far. The Redwood den was closer to the Centrals than any of the other dens. And that was something that I was grateful for. Adalyn had a longer drive, but I would go with her. I wouldn't let her do this alone. And both of us would ensure Cole wouldn't be doing this alone either. The moon goddess had said that he needed us, so we would be there.

And then again, maybe I needed them as well.

I'd had literal middle child syndrome sometimes, and I needed to get over it.

Instead of getting into my car, which I had left at the Central den, I used this time to let my magic flow through me and let my wolf to the surface. Though I was still running in human form, I needed to run it all.

I was a runner and a soldier, a wolf and a witch. I used the magic of my mother's line to use the earth to run faster. And yet sometimes, it wasn't always enough. While on this run, I could use it to keep on alert just in case a vampire slid through any of the den territory not protected by wards. Because we shared our space with humans now more than ever, and we didn't have as much magic as we had a century ago. The den was protected by the wards, the magic that flowed through the witches, the moon goddess, and the Pack bonds themselves. It was a delicate balance with the way that magic had changed with the current war.

The territories of the four Packs in our alliance were done by marking. So I knew when I went from one territory to the next, or if I slid through neutral zones that we all took care of. Located just outside the Central den, the main neutral area was where we met with each of the Pack's leaders. The Aspens had the furthest travel but had the largest territory. Mostly because the previous Alpha had been hoarding power and magic. Now Chase, the Aspen Alpha, was doing his best to share the resources even though they didn't have the people or the magic they had before. All because of an Alpha gone rogue. Much like the former Central Alpha.

I used my magic to press against the earth, the balls of my feet heating up as magics burned, and I moved faster than any other wolf could. It was an odd little trick I had learned as a pup, something that had surprised and probably scared my parents. But then our Alpha, my uncle, had run with me, and though eventually he couldn't keep up, he had done his best and had taught me to use my own skills.

Not all of my siblings could do this. In fact, none of them could do it the way I could. It had made me feel a little bit special in a Pack where everyone seemed to be special.

But I knew the Centrals didn't have members like my family. They didn't have pyrokinetics or sensates. They didn't have the magic that we did, or I had. But I was Central now. And I needed to get that idea into my head.

I kept moving, wondering what the moon goddess had been thinking. Maybe if we had figured it out beforehand she wouldn't have forced it on us. And then again, maybe we wouldn't have. I just didn't know, and it was all a little worrying.

I made it to the Central den and nodded at the sentry.

"Nico. Oh, I guess, should I call you Alpha's mate?" Rory, a kind man with gray eyes, asked. He was one of the sentries, a soldier like I had been. We had trained together a few times, though I usually trained with my own Pack members. I knew that Cole trained with Chase, and Adalyn trained with Cassius and several other Aspen Pack members.

I didn't know what we would do now, but we would all have to find new ways. Because everything had changed in an instant, and we had not been prepared.

"Just call me Nico. I'm still trying to figure this out."

"So are the rest of us, but we like you, Nico. And Adalyn. Although we don't know her as well."

I smiled. "I think Adalyn is going to fit into this role quite nicely."

I didn't mention myself because I wasn't sure how. I barely knew how to use my own magics, but I would try to find a way to help the Centrals.

I moved towards the wards, the magic touching me. I inhaled, the shocking breath new. This wasn't the same slight pain that came from going into a den that wasn't my own. Instead, this was a welcoming embrace. My den. One that called to me and wanted me.

It shocked me that this was mine. A sense of home began to slide over me.

My eyes widened, but before I stepped foot further into the den wards, the earth moved beneath my feet.

It wasn't my magic this time, and as I turned, Rory's face went bloodless and everything went dark.

The earth pushed me, my own magic scrolling around me as I landed on all fours and tossed my bag to the side. I moved towards Rory as he clutched his side, blood pouring between his fingers.

"Bomb. It's the black magic bomb."

Vampires. Damn it.

I pressed my hand to his side. The Central Healer ran up to me. Lane, a small woman with dark eyes, nodded at me. "Go. Others will need our help. The children were coming home from school."

This time the blood drained from my face, and I ran, trusting Rory with the Healer's touch. If she hadn't been close by, on her own patrol, it would've been fatal. But I needed to go, needed to find those pups. Other soldiers were moving, but then another bomb exploded, and I knew the vampires weren't here to just play.

My watch buzzed, and I looked down, an alert saying that the Aspens were also under attack.

I cursed under my breath, knowing Adalyn was there.

But I could still feel her along the mating bond; she had to be fine. Cole was there too, now that I thought about it, and my eyes turned cold, but I closed my eyes for an instant, touching the bond ever so slightly.

Both bonds flared for an instant, and I felt warmth back.

They were alive and checking on me.

Dear God, was this what it meant to be mated? It was an odd feeling, and I didn't feel ready.

But I didn't have time to think about it. I moved forward as a vampire slid out of the darkness, his eyes bright red, his fangs elongated. This one was just at the edge of control, still young enough to be piloted by someone else, but with its own tenacity that it could make its own decisions if it thought hard enough.

I cursed under my breath as I saw the van on its side. The pups had been coming home from school, the Central den too small to have its own. It had always been safe in the past. But it wasn't this time. And I knew if those pups were gone, if Cole had lost the children of his Pack because they had used the city's schools like they always had, I didn't think my mate would survive.

The vampire threw another bomb, and I shoved my foot down onto the ground, my magic pouring from me. A wave of earth and soil and roots and other plant material shoved up from the ground and smothered the vampire, taking the bomb with it. It exploded, the shock wave knocking me off my feet. I hit the ground with a thud, but kept moving, rolling to my feet as I made it towards the van. The pups were crying, but I didn't smell blood. I moved, ripping the door off the frame as four little pups, ages four through eight, looked up at me with wide eyes.

The adult, a man named Matthew, lay nearby, passed out but not bleeding. Underneath him was another pup, a small one whimpering, but he had thrown himself over them, protecting them. And now, the little pups were doing the same to him.

"Strong little guys, aren't you," I whispered. "Okay. Come with me. You know who I am."

"Alpha's mate," the littlest said, as I moved forward and gathered them out of the van. I knew that I had stopped that one vampire from throwing the third bomb. But for all I knew there were others. The earth had taken the impact, and so had my magic.

I let the pups crawl all over me as the others came. I had only gotten here faster because of my magic. As two familiar people ran out from between the trees, my feet almost went out from beneath me and my heart shuddered.

"Nico?" Cole asked as he ran, gathering up the children as he did. Adalyn was there too, kneeling down beside a now waking Matthew.

"The babies are fine. Aren't you?"

"We are, Alpha's mate," the littlest girl said, fluttering her eyelashes.

I laughed, surprising myself that I could do so despite such fear, and kissed the top of her head.

"Okay now. You are a flirt."

"Mommy says so." She leaned against me, sniffing at my neck, and Cole just met my gaze.

He was smiling, but I knew the fear and anger warred within him. I could feel it along the bond, the same with Adalyn as she helped Matthew up.

Others were there then, the blood covering Lane's hands fresh. "Rory's fine." The question in my eyes as Cole turned to her.

"Help Matthew if you can."

Lane nodded. "Of course, Alpha. I might need a little more power."

"Can I help with that?" Adalyn asked, frowning.

Lane shook her head. "I don't know yet. For now, let's just use Cole's, and then I'll see if I can use the two of you. Having three Alphas to help boost my power would be a nice thing."

And as I looked between my two mates, I thought that maybe that was why this had happened. Why the bonds had come so quickly.

We had almost lost the children today. Almost lost a friend.

And the war wasn't over.

Cole

My wolf slammed into me and I reined it back in, reminding myself I was the Alpha. I had to be stronger than this, even though all I wanted to do was rage.

The vampire horde had come to us, had hurt our children, had hurt the Aspens, and had threatened my mates.

In the end, the children ended up with a few bruises that were easily healed by our Healer. And while I tried my best not to think too hard on the idea that we could have lost our future, I had to swallow the bile rising in my throat of the thought that Nico had been so close.

He had thrown himself bodily into protecting the children of the Pack.

In the eyes of the Centrals, Nico and Adalyn were unknowns. Yes, they knew of them as warriors, as good fighters, but they didn't know of them as Alphas. *We* didn't know of them. I didn't know how I would be as a mate, let alone having two Alpha's mates who were supposed to help me. Was that what an Alpha's mate did? I didn't know. I hadn't had an Alpha growing up. I hadn't had an Alpha's mate.

Maybe that's why I felt like I was floundering.

And that Nico and Adalyn were going to fall down with me.

But no, they had nearly been killed. Adalyn with the Aspens, Nico here on our land. If Nico hadn't done magic I had never seen him do before, he would've died. The children would've died, and I would've lost my mate in one blink.

My wolf raged, wanting to howl, and I sucked in the strength again, reminding myself I needed to breathe. To focus.

"Cole, are you there?"

I looked up at the video feed to see Chase and Cruz standing there. Chase, the Alpha of the Aspens, and Cruz, the Heir, were first and second in command when it came to the Aspen Pack. While Chase, like me, held most of the mantle of the power of the Pack—individual bonds connecting us to each Pack member—Cruz, like my Heir, held part of the power in order to ease the burden on the Alpha's shoulders.

I knew that Chase's new mate had done the same for him, and somehow Nico and Adalyn would find a way to do the same for me. I wasn't quite sure how it would happen, only that it would, because everyone kept telling me.

I didn't know what I was doing, and I didn't think they did either, but we would figure it out. We didn't have another choice.

"I'm here. Sorry."

"The damage to the land was minimal," Cruz continued, looking down at his tablet with the notes from our previous attack. "We have two injuries, Ronin and Triton. They'll be fine though; our Healer was able to work on them quickly without using much of her strength."

I nodded. "We almost lost two of ours, and the children had a few bumps and bruises, but Nico was able to get to them in time."

Chase's mouth quirked into a small smile. "Your mates are helpful. Strong. It's good for your Pack, Cole."

I let out a small growl, not sure why I was angry, beyond the obvious. "I'm tired of this. I'm tired of not being able to find my way."

Chase gave Cruz a look, and the other man nodded at me before walking out of the room, leaving us two Alphas alone.

"While Cruz is our friend, I figured you might want an Alpha-to-Alpha talk right now."

I sighed and ran my hands through my hair. "How do

you deal with this? Nico was almost killed in front of me, and if Adalyn and I weren't already heading towards here, she would've been hurt, too. I don't understand how you can handle this. How you can handle Skye being hurt."

Chase growled, low and menacing. "I didn't handle it very well, remember? I almost lost her before, but I have to trust in her strength. And while it's odd to say, I have to trust in the moon goddess. Because we have to survive this."

"How can I trust something that throws me off the deep end?" I whispered, worried that I even voiced those fears. "Have you ever heard of a mating like ours?"

Chase shook his head. "No, but we don't know all the histories of every Pack. We have more connections now than we did in the past, but we've been insular. And I'm not just talking about the Aspen Pack. All of us have been cut off from others to the point that we lost who we were for a long time. We needed to be that way, to keep our secrets from the humans. But now the humans know us, and they're scared."

"And not only of us," I added.

"You're right. They're scared of what the vampires want. People are being snatched off the streets. Not just humans. Witches and shifters alike."

"What do you think Valac is up to?" I asked.

Chase pinched the bridge of his nose. "Nothing good. We killed his mate. What would you do if someone came after yours?"

A low growl filled the room, and I realized it was coming from me.

Chase cursed under his breath. "Sorry. You're new in your mating, so any idea of a threat will cause you to do that."

"You say that as if you wouldn't gut someone for coming after yours."

Chase sighed. "True. And we're not insane like that vampire."

"I don't know what's going to happen," I added. "I don't know what Valac wants, other than our deaths."

"And if he can't get at the Aspens, he'll attack our allies."

I sighed. "And the one that he thinks is the weakest."

"Don't. You're not weak."

"No, we're not. My Pack is strong, and we're only getting stronger, but we're also not as strong as the other Packs in the area. In his eyes, we are the weakest." I narrowed my gaze. "And that means they'll be in for a surprise when they try to come after us."

"Like that witch and wolf hybrid of yours," Chase added, and I smiled.

"My mate has hidden talents."

Chase threw his head back and laughed. "You let those hidden talents do what they need to. I don't need to know." He chuckled but the smile quickly fell from his face. "Seriously though, are you okay?"

"The Pack? We're figuring it out. Me? I think my answer's the same."

The other Alpha sighed. "The humans are worried, the witches are crumbling, and we need to be strong. We can do that. We're allies. We're friends. You're like my brother."

My lips twitched. "I guess I'll have to deal with that."

Chase flipped me off and we said our goodbyes. I was exhausted since I hadn't slept well the night before. Adalyn and Nico had slept by my sides, and the three of us had just cuddled in a puppy pile, not touching one another for anything more than comfort. My house wasn't big enough for the three of us, and I was unprepared for a mate. Let alone two. It felt like everything in my entire life was something I wasn't prepared for. I hadn't expected to be Alpha either, but here I was, leading, and feeling as if I should probably know what the hell I was doing.

I made my way out of my office and inhaled that sweet scent that I knew was only one person.

Nico looked up from his phone and gave me a quelling look. "You okay?"

"People keep asking me that, and yet you were the one in a battle."

"And I'm all healed. Breathe, okay? I can't focus on what I need to do if you keep stressing about me stubbing my toe."

I growled and moved forward, cupping the back of his neck as he got up from the couch.

"You didn't fucking stub your toe. You were nearly killed."

"But I wasn't."

"No, you weren't." I let out a shaky breath and pressed my forehead to his. I've never seen that magic before, Nico. And I only caught the tail end of it."

Nico shrugged and pulled away. I knew it was because he was thinking, not because he was rejecting me, and I forced my wolf to understand that. He didn't understand the intricacies of that right then, though.

"My mother is the most powerful earth witch that I know. She can do that type of magic in her sleep. I don't have that strength, but I'm learning. I don't have it through my hands, though. It's mostly through my feet, which I always found hilarious."

My lips twitched. "So you stomp on the ground and make the earth move?"

"Sometimes. And sometimes I do indeed stub my toe."

"I don't like the idea that the vampires are getting so close. That we can't find where Valac is hiding now."

"I talked to Cruz earlier about our scouts, and you're right. It's odd to think they're using magic to keep us away."

"That's the only thing that I can think of." I paused. "Are you and Cruz close?"

I hadn't meant to voice the words or let the jealousy slide through. Nico had friends, just like I did. Hell, I had just spoken to Cruz. And yet, for some reason, my wolf wasn't happy with the fact that Cruz and Nico were talking. There was something seriously wrong with me.

Nico rolled his eyes. "I don't do well with the whole jealous wolf thing. I know we're newly mated, and we're still figuring each other out. But don't. Cruz is just a friend, and we've never fucked. Does that help?"

Based on the crude words falling from his lips, I knew he was a little angry. I didn't blame him.

"I'm sorry."

"I'm sorry that I get growly whenever you talk to Chase. And he's mated to my cousin."

"We are becoming one big happy family, aren't we?" I asked with a laugh.

"A dysfunctional one that's trying to stand against tyranny, but here we are." Nico began to pace the living room. "Adalyn is training with Cassius and Audrey on the Aspen grounds right now. She had already promised them that she would be there before our mating, so she didn't want to break that engagement. But I know we're trying to find a balance between our former lives and whatever life that the moon goddess has sent us."

I turned to him then, moved forward, and brushed his hair from his face. "Are you finding your balance? What can I do to make it easier?"

Nico leaned into my touch and my wolf wanted to purr like a cat.

"I don't know, Cole. You have all this stress and worry and power on your shoulders, and I like the fact that I could be the person that you could lean on. Adalyn has so much raw energy within her that she practically vibrates with it. She's a leader, and this role was meant for her. I could sense it. I think she's the bridge that could truly connect the Centrals and Aspens."

"And you, Nico? What about the Redwoods?"

"The Redwoods have always been there for the new Centrals."

I noticed him use the word 'new,' considering the former Centrals had nearly decimated the Redwood Pack.

"It's hard to think when you're around, Nico," I whispered.

His lips twitched. "There's something I can do about that. To relieve the tension. Because you look tense, Alpha."

Nico's hand slid over my shoulders, squeezing, and I groaned.

"I didn't realize that I was so tight."

We both looked at each other and burst out laughing.

"Oh, you're tight."

I growled and slid my hand down Nico's back to cup him. "Oh. I think it's my turn. Don't you think?"

His eyes glowed gold, the wolf at the forefront. I knew mine were doing the same. I lowered my face to his, capturing his lips in a sweet, innocent caress before we growled into each other. And then it was no-holds-barred.

This wasn't just the mating urge flowing between us. This wasn't just the moon goddess. Nico was my friend.

Friend first, lover next. I'd always admired him, always wanted him. And now he was mine. And I was trying to figure out what to do with that.

We growled against one another, tearing at each other's clothes to get each other skin to skin.

"You taste sweet," Nico rasped against my lips. I tugged on his hair, and then we were tumbling to the ground.

"I need you in my mouth," I growled, and I slithered down his body, cupping his cock in my hands.

"You're so fucking thick. No wonder you stretched me."

Nico grinned and folded his hands behind his head.

"Oh, you just have all the fun that you want, Alpha mine. I'm going to lie back and think of England."

I growled. "You better think of me." And then I swallowed him whole.

He tasted of musk and heat, and he bucked into my mouth as I let him hit the back of my throat. I hollowed my cheeks and moved, cupping his balls in my hand as I continued to work him. I licked, and I sucked, enjoying the way that he filled my mouth. "Alpha. Stop. I'm going to come."

That was the idea, but I couldn't say that out loud, considering his dick was in my mouth. So I continued to suck and lick until I pulled back and grinned up at him. His eyes were still glowing gold, his claws out as he dug them into the carpet.

"Don't fuck up my floors."

Nico grinned. "Our floors."

I growled before I sucked him down again, giving him all my attention. And when he tightened again, I hollowed my cheeks and swallowed him as he came, groaning my name.

Somehow I found myself on my back, letting him kiss me and take control just for an instant as I tried to hold back my own climax. I wanted to come right then on his stomach, but first, there were a few things I needed to do. Namely, lick and touch him again.

He slid his hands down between us, sliding his hand over my dick, then between my cheeks. He played with me, and I shook my head, pulling away.

"Oh no you don't. I'm Alpha here."

Nico swallowed hard and nodded. "Whatever you say, Cole."

That moment between us the bond flickered with heat.

This could be my future. Mine. I didn't know what I had done in the past for the goddess to bless me, even if she had surprised me in every way possible, but this was my future.

Mine.

A small part, a small piece, and it was everything.

Nico cupped my face and looked at me. "Are you okay?"

"With you? I am."

Nico's eyes glistened, my mate, swallowing hard before I kissed him softly and scrambled to my feet.

"What are you doing?" Nico asked.

I pulled him to his feet, kissed him hard on the mouth, and dragged him to the bedroom. "We're going to have to start keeping lube in every room of the house."

Nico threw his head back and laughed before I shoved him on the bed and pulled the lube out of the nightstand.

I poured it onto my hands and then onto my cock, before I slowly worked him between his legs.

He groaned, looking like a golden god in front of me.

He was so beautiful, so powerful, and he was mine.

I didn't know what would come next, how we would defeat Valac and the others. Or the lingering magic that came from the coven.

Or the darkness that came from the demon that we still hadn't seen.

But right at that moment, the only thing that mattered was right in front of me.

So I positioned myself between my mate's legs and looked down at him.

"Are you ready?"

Nico nodded. "For you? Always."

And I moved, breaching his entrance as we both groaned.

He was tight, easing back on me as both of us became sweat-slick, shaking. But as he enveloped me, I sucked in a breath, knowing that this was part of my forever. It was chaos, a cacophony of beauty. And mine.

Once I was fully seated, I gripped his now newly hard cock and thrust. We both groaned, his cock twitching in my hand as he slid his hand over mine, and we moved.

The bond between us flared, my wolf stretching, wanting its mate. And when he tightened around me, coming over his belly, I followed, filling him up.

The bond strengthened, my mate, becoming mine in truth.

I hadn't asked for this. I hadn't known it could be possible.

But I knew that no matter what happened, Nico would be my rock. The one I could lean on.

I kissed him softly, knowing that I didn't have an ounce of an idea of what could happen next.

"Breathe, Alpha," Nico said softly as I slid out of him. He winced before he kissed me. "I've got you. Just breathe for a minute. Let me take the burden."

And as a bond-formed crevice opened in my heart, my soul, I leaned against him and let everything that had happened wash over me, and let Nico hold me.

Something I'd never done before.

And I was afraid if I did again, I would break him.

But I let him hold me. If only for the moment.

CHAPTER
EIGHT

Adalyn

"So, when is the mating ceremony?" Lily asked, and I shook my head, trying to keep up.

This was the first time I had been able to spend an afternoon with the women in my life, my friends, for what felt like ages. We were all a little bit busy figuring out exactly how I had found myself mated to not one but two men, and dealing with the vampire horde.

"You're going to stress her out." Audrey shook her head. She was the Beta of the Aspens and my best friend. It was odd to think we wouldn't live next to each other any longer.

Then again, she was newly mated to Gavin, and things had changed with them as well.

Skye just laughed. "You know Lily. She needs answers." My former Alpha's mate fluttered her eyelashes and I met her gaze. She had always been able to meet my gaze, even before she had been mated to Chase. That was because of who she was within the hierarchy. Now we held the same positions within our new Packs. It was as if her thoughts were along the same lines as mine because she smiled warmly and gripped my hand.

"We'll have an Alphas' mates meeting. Along with my aunt and cousin."

I narrowed my gaze, remembering who exactly had mated each of the local Alphas. "It seems that the Jamensons are wheedling their ways into every part of the Pack Alpha structure. Considering your other cousin is one of my mates."

Mates.

That was a word I wasn't used to.

And my wolf wanted to preen and prowl around the den so all would know.

The human part of me was beyond confused.

Skye just beamed. "I told you we were taking over the world. One Pack at a time. We don't need war, just love."

My heart did that twisting sensation because I didn't love them. Not in the way I should. Not yet.

I cared for them. I respected them. The two men that were now my mates were my friends. But I didn't love them. And I wasn't sure I could trust a moon goddess that took that choice from me. It would have been nice to have the idea of a mate.

"What are you thinking? You look sad now," Dara asked as she settled more firmly onto the couch. There were dark circles under her eyes, and I knew she had to be exhausted. She was putting so much of her time and energy and self into the den wards and trying to find a cure for that dark, jagged magic that the vampires wielded. I gave Skye a look, and she nodded tightly, as did Audrey. I knew that they would be talking to Dara about it again.

The only person that could make Dara do anything was Cruz, at least that had been true in the past. Now they were too busy growling and sniping at one another to actually listen to each other. That was something else that had been on my list to talk about with my friends to try to fix. But was it my right? They weren't my Pack any longer. Did I have the right to try to fix the inner workings of a den?

"You have sad face again."

I looked up at Wren and cringed.

"I'm sorry. I'm just thinking about how things have changed, and it's weird. I'm afraid that I'm going to lose my connections with you guys. I don't know the members of the Centrals that well. There aren't even many. And I don't want to lose my friendships. Or lose the right to bully Dara into taking care of herself." I growled as I said it and she flipped me off, even as she smiled.

"Now that was a truth I've been waiting to hear," Novah said softly into the silence as we stared at one another. Considering Novah was a Truth Seeker, I figured that that was more than just relief in her tone.

"What makes you think we'll let you get away from us?" Audrey asked.

"Because we're not. You might be the new Alpha's mate of the Central Pack, along with Nico, but you're still part of ours. We won't let you go totally."

"I still have connections to the Redwoods even though it might not be metaphysical anymore," Skye put in. "I have responsibilities to this den, and I've made friends and will continue to make friends with those within this den. But I didn't walk away from my relationships and past. You don't have to, either. There's a place with both dens. Believe me. All of you told me over and over again that these four Packs were becoming one in this alliance. Well, now I'm telling you. You're not getting rid of us. You're gaining mates, responsibility, power, connections. And I bet you there are people within the Central Pack that could use a friend. They could use a protector. The moon goddess may annoy us sometimes by not being exactly open in what she wants, but she's not wrong."

I frowned. "I don't like everything being so sudden."

"And with the way you three have been growling around each other, maybe it's not too sudden at all," Wren whispered.

I winced. "Was it that obvious?"

Novah laughed. "Just a little."

Dara picked up her phone and frowned. "Wynter was supposed to be here but is stuck at work. I'm sorry."

I shook my head, thinking of the human that was a Pack member but spent more time outside the den than not these days. Much like the Central Pack members did.

"Maybe I should talk with Wynter to see how she likes living within two worlds. Because that's sort of what the Centrals do."

I didn't want to break confidences or talk about anything secret within my den, my new one. But I also needed help. And why not ask my friends?

"You could. I know that it used to be that not all of the Pack members lived within the den. It was easier to keep it secret if you didn't have a group of people all stationed in one area. And then things changed with the first war," Audrey added.

Skye leaned forward. "My parents' generation lived within the den and had apartments and houses outside it. It just depended on what their job was. And what was needed."

"I don't know. I just feel like I am grasping at straws here, trying to find my place." I sighed. "Then again, sometimes I felt like I was doing that here. At least after the shift when Blade died."

Audrey gripped my hand. "I always thought it weird that you weren't the Enforcer. Yes, Steele is amazing at what he does, and he is where he needs to be, but part of me also thought that you would have been perfect for it. Or even a higher lieutenant. I don't know. Then again, there was a reason. You couldn't be the Alpha's mate and Alpha in your own right if you held another title within another den."

"And I'm pretty sure that Steele would get all growly if you took his mantle from him," Wren put in and I laughed, thinking of the growly Enforcer who was in charge of the outside protection of the den. Considering everything that kept attacking the Pack, I knew he had a lot on his plate, and it had been my job at one point to help him with that. Now I was going to have to do it for the Centrals.

"It's more than that, though, isn't it?" Dara asked, tired but intuitive.

"What's more than that?" I stiffened.

"Your hesitance. Yes, it was sudden, but it was magic. Sometimes magic is sudden. Sometimes it's painstakingly slow, and it makes you want to gouge your own eyes out. But we're not talking about me."

Lily gripped Dara's hand and smiled softly. "I told you I'll help you. We'll work on a spell."

"I know. It's why you're one of my best friends. You and Wynter. You throw yourselves into everything."

"I try. Now, tell us what's wrong, Adalyn," Lily added.

"There's something I should have told you before." I met each of their gazes, these women who were my friends, my touchstones, that were no longer my Packmates, and swallowed hard. Then I told them of the man who could have been my first mate. The man who I felt had betrayed me.

Dara's eyes widened as Audrey cursed, and Skye and Wren's eyes began to fill. Novah frowned at me, then looked down at her hands.

"Why didn't I know? Why didn't my magic tell me?"

I looked at the Truth Seeker and shook my head. "Because you sense truths that are spoken. And I've never spoken that out loud here." I let out a shaky breath and looked at my best friend. "I'm sorry I didn't tell you. But it was around the time everything broke."

"I understand completely. Considering that I had to hide my own mate from you before because of our war, it makes sense. But I just really hope there's no more secret mating or rejections within this Pack. Okay?" She looked at everyone. All of them held up their hands and shook their heads.

"I'm happily mated, thank you," Novah added, as Skye nodded in agreement.

"I know what it feels like to be rejected," Lily put in, as she gripped my hand. "Not as a mate, but other things." She didn't elaborate, and she didn't need to. She would if she needed to later.

"But don't worry. We're your family now, just like those men are. And I'm so happy for you. Even though it's strange to think that you're not a Packmate anymore."

I laughed, even as emotions hit hard. I wasn't their

Packmate anymore. I was an *ally*. "Going through the wards to get here is so weird. They're welcoming me as if I'm coming to a previous home. But there's still that tingle of sensation, like you're going to a different Pack. You know what I mean?"

"I know exactly what you mean," Skye answered. "Considering I feel it every time I go to the Redwoods."

My wolf relaxed, knowing she was home in more than one place. I looked at all of my friends and smiled, then continued eating my snacks and listening to them talk about their lives. Because tonight wasn't only about me. It was about getting to know my friends again and knowing I had them to come home to. Even as I needed to remember to find new connections. I was the Alpha's mate. I had responsibilities, and I wanted to do good. After we finished our meals, we said our goodbyes, each of us having duties or other things to do for the night.

I walked outside of Audrey's home and smiled as Chase came up and kissed Skye hard on the mouth. The two Aspen Alphas growled at one another before Skye smacked her mate's ass and walked away to go off on patrol. Chase looked at me and I met his gaze. I blinked.

My wolf could meet his eyes.

As I grinned, Chase just rolled his own eyes. "Took you long enough to realize that, fellow Alpha. If we were at war with each other or trying to fight for our own dominance, it would be different. But our wolves respect and know one another. You're going to be a good Alpha's mate.

120

Believe that. Believe in yourself. And as you know, Cole and I are trying to figure this whole Alpha thing out together. So now the five of us can do it."

My wolf preened and I grinned, hugging him close. I moved back quickly though, before his scent could mark me, and he snorted. "Yeah, going home smelling like another man, even a happily mated one, is probably not good for someone as newly mated as you."

"Very much so. I need to head back. I want to see them. And find my place. And, of course, find a way to stop the vampires."

Chase growled, met my gaze, and nodded. "Drive safe. Do you want one of us to escort you home?"

I flipped him off as he laughed.

"Okay fine. Just stay on the neutral road. Our sentries are around."

"Of course. I helped my Enforcer settle our routes this morning."

Chase whistled beneath his teeth and then left to follow his mate.

See, that was one step towards figuring out my path, even if I felt like I had no idea what I was doing.

I said my goodbyes to others as I walked past, some giving me confused looks because they still didn't know what was going on. I didn't blame them. Things happened quickly, and while the rumor mill worked hard, it was all still so new.

I drove past the front gates and waved at the sentries,

the magic within the wards a caressing goodbye. It brought a tear to my eye, knowing that my own den remembered me. It might not exactly be sentient, but in my heart of hearts it felt like it. It wasn't that long of a drive towards the Central den, and I was missing my mates. I pressed the button on my steering wheel and cleared my throat.

"Text Cranky Alpha and Fast Foot that I'm coming home."

My car agreed, and I smiled, knowing I should probably change their names at some point. But I didn't want to.

The car pinged that someone had texted back, and I turned the corner, ready to hear whatever they had to say when the explosion hit.

A vampire bomb of black magic slammed into the side of my SUV and tossed it into the air. I held on and cursed as everything went by quickly and yet achingly slow. The SUV slammed onto its side and I hit my head on the door, glass shards digging into my skin as metal twisted and rubber burned. The SUV skidded along the grass beside the road, and I held on for dear life, hoping to hell that I didn't black out. Because I was alone out here; I didn't sense a sentry like I should.

The vampires were here, and this was bad.

As another bomb hit, I undid my seatbelt, wiped the blood from my eyes, and tried to crawl out of the SUV.

The car's computer was dead, and I reached for my phone, trying to text an alert to someone, but there was nothing. Someone gripped me by my arm and shoved me through my broken front windshield, glass cutting into my cheek and my arm as I went. I let out a sharp yelp and swung out, trying to hit whoever had attacked me, and I looked into the red gaze of the vampire who hated us most.

Valac.

"Here's the bitch I was looking for."

I kicked out, trying to hit him again, but another vampire wrapped his arms around me, holding me close. I threw my head up and howled, letting the wolf through, hoping someone would hear. It was a mournful howl, fear and anger. They had to hear me. I would not go down without a fight. But then Valac slashed out, using his claws against my face. Blood seeped down my jaw, and then there was nothing.

Just darkness and pain.

And my wolf whimpered.

CHAPTER
NINE

Valac

Valac paced the small clearing and tried to hold back a smile. The others needed him to be calm and collected for this. Though it wasn't the bitch wolf that they had all wanted, it was close.

His master was waiting and needed answers. There was only so much time before Valac would have to come to account for everything that had happened, but this, this would be a reward. To show those bloody wolves what they deserved.

"She's trussed up. We're ready." He nodded at his new second in command, knowing it wasn't his Sunny. His precious mate. His precious Sunny was gone. Because of them.

And while he couldn't have that Aspen bitch, he could take the Central one. She had been an Aspen after all.

The news had spread of this new triad of Alphas.

What kind of abomination were they? Three Alphas in one role? No, soon there would only be two because he would kill her. And the rest of the wolves would understand who controlled the power. They would feel the pain that Valac did. They didn't understand what they had unleashed when they had taken Sunny from him.

Valac walked out into the clearing, into the structure that had been erected for this very purpose.

His vampires surrounded them, along with all the dark magic that they could muster. No wolf would be able to get through easily. No shifter cunt would come into this land and touch what was his.

The werewolf bitch hung from a rope from the structure, her hands above her head, the rope digging into her flesh. Other barbs of metal dug into her skin, cuts and bruises from the accident as well as Valac's own claws covered her body. There was another rope around her neck, and as soon as Valac willed it, the ropes on her arms would be cut and she would hang. She would die, trussed up like a little werewolf turkey.

Valac's lips twitched, but he reminded himself that he needed to be sane for this.

His master was waiting. There needed to be answers soon or his master would call in a new general.

And that could not happen. Not when Sunny's murderers were allowed to live.

So Valac smiled at his new prey. She opened her eyes, realization of what exactly was about to occur coming into them.

Valac finally allowed himself to smile.

And the madness took over.

CHAPTER
TEN

Nico

I RUBBED THE BACK OF MY NECK, ANNOYED AT THE hairs standing on end. Why did everything feel off? Something was in the wind, the magic bubbling beneath my skin evident. I frowned and looked down at my feet, the earth rumbling beneath it. Just a natural rumble, what happened when the magic touched me as if it wanted to say hello. But it didn't feel off.

Then again, I didn't truly know what I was doing.

"What is it?" Cole asked as he came up to my side. We weren't touching, but we were standing closer than we would have in the past. We were doing that more often, being near one another, as if we had to touch one another, and yet also knew that if we did there wouldn't be any thinking going on.

I was still getting used to the fact that I was *allowed* to touch him. I was testing my own limits, just like he was.

"I'm not sure. It's as if the magic in my veins wants to tell me something, but I'm not very good at the whole listening part."

"How does that work? Your magic." Cole slid his hands through his hair. He always did that when he was nervous. I didn't know what he would have to be nervous about. I liked talking about my magic. Though I didn't have as much as my mother did, or any of the full witches I knew. I only had a touch of it, and I didn't need to be nervous about it.

Even if I knew that was a lie. Of course, I was nervous about it. I would never be able to join the coven the way that I was, not that I wanted to. But an invite would've been nice. And now I knew the coven was in the process of imploding under its new leadership. They weren't even letting new members come in. They were becoming so insular, not wanting to help the Packs or the humans or any witches not part of their inner crew, that they were becoming obsolete.

And once again, my mind whirled in a thousand different directions, and I wasn't focusing on the mate in front of me.

"Now you're lost in thought. What's going on, Nico?"

I shook my head, doing my best not to wallow in whatever the hell was going on right then. "Sorry. Woolgathering. I'm a magic user because of my mother."

"I love Hannah. She's one of the kindest people I know. She's helped the few witches that we have within the den lean into their craft."

"Let me guess, because the coven doesn't want to help?" I didn't like the bitterness in my tone, but I couldn't stop it. The current coven didn't want me at all. They didn't want my magic and didn't even consider me part witch.

The coven before that had welcomed me, though I hadn't used them to the fullest capabilities because I hadn't been ready. Now I couldn't.

"The former coven did. This new leadership? Not so much."

I nodded as Cole growled. "I don't know what we're going to do about that." I paused. "I guess it's something I can actually help with though, right? Since I'm a magic user and mated to an Alpha. Before, I had to *hope* that the ones in charge would deal with it."

Cole's lips twitched. "Well, that would be us now. And we're trying to deal with it. It's not like we've been sitting on our hands. But the coven is insular and not attacking us with bombs, so it's not like we are making it top priority."

I rubbed my chin. "Maybe it's something I can do. My mother can use spells and witchcraft to move the earth and bend it to her will in order to protect. She's a Healer.

My magic lets me move fast. I think it aids me in my shift as well."

In order to shift from human to animal and back was a difficult and arduous process. Bones broke, tendons tore. You literally transformed your body into a new being. It wasn't easy, and it was painful. I only knew a few shifters who could now shift in an instant. Most took minutes. I even knew a few latent wolves who couldn't make the shift completely. But things, like mating, were changing.

"I have the magic within me that marks me as Alpha. The way that I can feel every Pack member."

"I only have a small snippet of that as your mate. I can't imagine how much you hold."

Cole rubbed a fist over his chest. "It's a little weird to be able to feel every single Packmate and sometimes not know who is who right away." He frowned again and stared at me, his wolf in his gaze.

"What's wrong?" I asked, my wolf on alert.

"I don't think it's the Pack bonds."

That's when I felt it, the mating bond between the three of us shuddering.

I staggered as Cole gripped my elbow.

"Addy," I whispered. "Fuck."

"Go. Run as fast as you can. I'll follow behind you."

"You don't want to drive?" My wolf clawed at me, hating this hesitation, but I needed to make sure Cole was safe too. I couldn't leave him behind without knowing.

"We'll both be faster running, but you're the fastest

wolf I know. Get to her. I'll be right behind you." He crushed his lips to mine in a promise, and then I was going. I put all of my magic into it, using the earth itself to push against my feet. I ran as if the hell hounds themselves were on me, and maybe that was the case.

Adalyn was in pain—she was *dying*.

Someone was daring to take her from us.

As the howl echoed across the forest, I moved ever faster.

Because that was Addy.

My Addy.

And someone had fucking hurt her.

I jumped over a fallen log, hearing the others come after us. The sentries and other wolves on patrol were coming, but they couldn't catch me. No one could when I ran like this.

I needed to get to Adalyn.

I zeroed in on the bond that connected the three of us. Cole was on his way. I *knew* he was. He would bring the others and do what he did best; he would lead.

He would find us.

Meaning I had to do what I did best. Move fast. I would find her, protect her, until the others got there.

I was afraid Adalyn couldn't protect herself right then. That was what let the fear in. Adalyn was stronger than I was. Far more dominant, a better fighter. A better soldier. I might be faster than her, but she could take me down in an instant. That was why we were friends. I didn't care that she was stronger than me. I liked it.

If she was calling out for help? That's what scared me. So I moved, the scents of burnt rubber and crushed metal filling my nose. I cursed under my breath again and made my way around the clearing. I slid along blood in the dirt, Adalyn's scent hitting me full force.

My wolf whimpered before it growled and I looked around, on edge.

My chest heaved, the strength it had taken for me to run as fast as I had caught up to me.

Only Adalyn wasn't here. Yet the vampire scent was.

Her SUV lay on its side, the bottom torn out by an explosion of some sort. Black metal shards dug into the metal casing and I knew it was the result of a vampire bomb. Something we were trying to eradicate. I would damn well put it to the top of my list once I found Adalyn.

We needed magic to do it, and if the coven wasn't going to help, then I was going to fucking do it myself. My mate was hurt. That was her blood on the ground, but I still felt her along the mating bond. So she was alive, and I was going to find her.

And damn anyone who got in my way.

I inhaled, trying to follow the scent and hunt her down.

I wasn't a Tracker by nature, not like my brother or my friends. But I was still good at this. I would find her.

I let out a solitary howl to let Cole know I was okay and where I was, and then I continued to move.

I followed the trail, the scent increasing as I got closer, the fact that her blood was brushed along some of the fallen leaves disheartening. My Adalyn was hurt.

And they had dragged her.

And she hadn't fought back.

I held back the growl because that meant she had to be unconscious.

My Addy would not go down without a fight, no matter what happened.

I kept moving, slower this time as I got closer. I could hear the sounds of vampires moving about now. My howl had hopefully alerted Cole and the others where I was, but not the vampires. I did it just at the right decibel that it should have worked. Then again, we didn't know exactly how sensitive the vampires' hearing was. But it was the only thing I could do. Well, not exactly. I pulled out my phone and texted.

Me: *They have her. She's alive.*

Cole: *Do you see her?*

Me: *I'm almost there. Are you close?*

Cole: *I'm behind you.*

I knew he didn't mean directly because I couldn't scent him, but I kept moving, kept getting closer. It sounded as if there were at least thirty vampires around, and I wouldn't be able to fight them all, not and keep Adalyn close. Rage filled me, pushed at me, and my wolf wanted to fight, but I was smarter than that. I wasn't going to sacrifice myself and still end up with Adalyn dead. I would be smart about this, even though nothing about me wanted to remain smart in that moment.

I kept close to the ground, knowing if I needed to shift, I'd have to do it quickly, pulling on the last reserves of my magic to do so.

I scented Cole before I heard him and looked over my shoulder to see him coming at me. He was shirtless, sweat slicking his skin. I knew he ran full out. He gestured with his hands and told me that there were four others around us, waiting, and I knew more would come as well.

With those odds, I thought we could make it.

I nodded tightly and kept moving, following the bond and her scent.

What I saw nearly made me throw up.

Adalyn was there. Strung up by her arms, and her neck, blood pouring from wounds on her side and on her face. They had cut her, had hurt her.

My mate. Our mate.

She was still unconscious. The vampires milled about around her, her feet at least ten feet above the ground, but I knew who stood closest. Who smiled up at her.

Valac.

I looked at Cole and he nodded tightly before holding up his hand and moving. I followed, my Alpha in charge. Cruz, the Aspen Heir, came from my right, and I knew he had run from the Aspen side. I was glad for it because he was one of the strongest fighters I knew.

Cruz took out the first vampire before there was even a sound. And then it was on. We had to stop them from cutting that last rope before Adalyn ended up hanging by her neck. She wouldn't survive that, and no one around us would survive because I would kill all of them if she was hurt any further. I moved, slicing my claws through the neck of the nearest vampire. It fell before it let out a single sound, and then I killed the next, and then the next. Cole killed four vampires in one blow, his rage balanced on a knife's edge. I knew if we weren't careful, we could turn rogue. That was the anger pounding through us, but I ignored that worry and I jumped. Using the last remaining remnants of my magic, I pushed myself off the ground, using the earth magic to grip the branch that Adalyn was tied to, and sliced through the rope at her neck. If she fell now, she would survive. Broken but survivable.

Cole was there then, fighting Valac, claw for claw. Fear erupted through me, but I had to focus on Adalyn. I had to keep her safe.

She looked up, finally waking. Her eyes widened and she growled, her eyes now glowing gold with her wolf.

"Cut the rope. Let me fall."

"Damn it. You'll be hurt."

"I might not be a cat, but I can fall. My legs aren't broken. I can do this, Nico. Trust me."

I wanted to grip her closer, to gather her in my arms

and never let anyone hurt her, but if I did that, she would never trust me. She had to fight for herself. And with the way that her hands were tied, she couldn't break through the ropes on her own. We'd yell at each other later because I was not happy about this.

I growled again then sliced through the rope but kept ahold of it. She dropped a few feet and glared up at me before I let her roll to the ground and back up. Without her weight on the ropes, she was able to tear through them quickly and sliced out the jugular of the nearest vampire. I jumped and rolled off the tree and killed the next vampire, but as we began to circle Valac, the vampire general just smiled at us.

"This isn't the end. Not for your bitch, not for any of this." He threw down a shard of black magic, and I threw myself over Adalyn. She would hate me in the morning, but at least she'd be alive to be angry. Dark angular shards of magic slid into my skin, and I ignored it as others shouted and moved around.

I knew as soon as I looked up Valac would be gone, but Adalyn was alive.

My *mate* was alive.

Cole was there, holding both of us, and I swallowed hard, knowing we needed a Healer.

Knowing we needed retribution.

Our Adalyn was safe, but now we had a hell of a lot more questions than we did answers.

Cole

My wolf felt as if it was going to rip through my skin, needing to escape. To tear through anybody who dared to come after its mate.

Adalyn had almost died. Had almost bled out in our arms after she had hung for who knows how long.

Valac was going to die for many reasons. But this one? This was the deepest cut.

"Calm yourself," Nico whispered as I looked over at my other mate. Even though he looked anything but calm.

We were on our way back to the den, Adalyn between us, sucking in deep breaths as she held each of our hands.

"Is Wren on her way?" she asked, wincing as we hit a

bump. This was the fastest way to get her there even while injured, and I hated the fact that she was still in pain.

I met Nico's gaze over her head and leaned forward. "Lane is our Healer, Adalyn. She's on her way to the den now. She was in the city helping with the birth of one of our human Packmates."

Adalyn turned to me, pain-filled gaze narrowing. "Crap. I forgot. I'm sorry. Did Sasha have the baby?" she asked.

I nodded. "She did. In the human hospital, thanks to complications. Lane is on her way back though. She'll meet us at the den and she'll help heal you. You'll be fine."

She squeezed my hand and nodded. "Of course, I will be. Lane is great at what she does. I think I just have a headache and I thought of Wren first. She's been my Healer for the past few years. I got confused."

I nodded and kissed the top of her head softly. I didn't want to harm her by touching her too roughly. But another part of me wanted to throw caution to the wind and gather her in my arms and never let her go. From the look on Nico's face, his thoughts were along the same lines.

Cruz drove, so we could sit in the back of the vehicle together. I had no idea why the Aspen Pack member had decided to be our chauffeur, but I didn't mind. My Pack members and other Aspens were back at the site with the vampires, dealing with the remains and searching for Valac.

I still couldn't believe the vampire had gotten out of

our hands. It made no damn sense to me. How was he so fast?

"Stop blaming yourself for him getting away," Adalyn put in.

I glared at her. "I didn't say any of that out loud, did I?" I asked.

"No, but I can see it on your face. Same as Nico's. The vampires are using magic that's stronger than ours because it is so dark. With each spell so dark, your soul is twisted around darkness more and more. You give up part of yourself to use magic like that and it ends up killing innocents around you long before you end up ending yourself. That's not the type of magic we're going to use. So don't blame yourself." She let out an oof as we hit a bump. She was still bleeding, even though we had patched her up as much as possible.

I glared at Cruz through the rearview mirror, and he sighed. "I'm sorry. That last storm wiped out part of this road. Pack members are on it."

"Just be careful."

"Don't grumble at Cruz because you're feeling surly."

"I'm feeling surly because my mate almost died, and I didn't know about it until we felt you through the bond."

"You felt that? I tried to do what I could, but I'm new at this."

"That whole bond thing works then?" Cruz asked, interest in his voice.

"Apparently," Adalyn answered, sounding more like

her old self with the other man. I was doing my best not to feel jealous, but it was difficult when a single wolf was talking to my mate when she was hurt.

Cruz cleared his throat, and that's when I realized I was growling.

"Settle down, Alpha. I don't want your woman. You don't need to add more aggression to the room."

"No, it's not just him," Nico mumbled, and Adalyn rested her head on my shoulder. My wolf calmed somewhat, even though it needed to be with her. Needed her to be safe.

"I'll be okay. You got to me in time."

I wanted to do anything but just sit there and wait to reach the den.

If Adalyn hadn't been hurt, I would have stayed with Chase and the others at the site. But I had left, same as Nico, because we hadn't been able to let Adalyn out of our sight. All newly mated wolves understood that, but I hated myself for letting down my Pack. Just like I hated the fact that I had let down Adalyn.

She mumbled something under her breath, and thankfully we made our way through the wards as she did. Her shoulders relaxed as if the magic of the den itself, albeit as small as it was, helped her to breathe again.

Cruz gritted his teeth up front but kept moving. The Healer's home and clinic was nearby, so Cruz pulled in swiftly as Lane ran out of the building, Jacqueline on her heels.

"Bring her inside." Lane looked through the open door at us. "Can you walk, Adalyn?" Lane asked. But before she could answer, I was out of the SUV and Nico was handing Adalyn to me.

Lane rolled her eyes and muttered something about Alphas, but I chose to ignore her. My mate was hurt. There was no way I was going to let her walk anywhere unassisted.

Maybe not for years at this point. If I had any say about it, she'd be locked in her room or have countless bodyguards by her side no matter what.

Nico grunted, and I had a feeling my possessiveness went through the bonds. Adalyn didn't stir in my arms, and that worried me more than anything. Because Adalyn always moved. She was a force. She would never let me put her in protection like that. If anything, she'd be the one who wanted to protect me.

Lane went to work as Adalyn woke up again, and I could feel the bond between Healer and Alpha grow. And it wasn't just because Lane was using the magic at that moment. No, it was because I now had more power. I had two mates, and that changed everything. Lane blinked for an instant before she smiled, and I knew she realized what was going on. We were stronger because of my mates. The moon goddess had forced this on us.

I had to hope to hell that that meant we were doing the right thing. Following along the path that she set before us. Then again, I wanted this.

I was afraid to say it out loud, but I wanted this. I wanted these two mates more than anything in the world. And I'd almost lost one of them today.

"Do you want to hear what happened?" Adalyn asked, as Lane began to work on the cuts on her face. I held back a growl, the sight of Adalyn's soft skin hurt, marred, making me want to growl. But I held back so I wouldn't scare Lane or the others. I needed to be in control.

"What happened exactly?" I asked, letting out a deep breath. My wolf needed to stop pushing me. Though I didn't think it was going to listen to me just then.

"I was on my way back from meeting with the girls in the Aspen Pack. There was no sign of anyone around other than the sentries." She paused and looked at me. "Are they okay?"

I nodded tightly. "Two were knocked out, but there wasn't enough time for anyone to notice that they were out and down for the count before you were taken."

She nodded before she winced, Lane having worked on her side. I held out my hand, and Adalyn slid hers into mine, Nico grabbing her other hand. My wolf calmed at that, the mating bond between the three of us settling.

"It's so weird that that feels better," she mumbled and Nico smiled.

"I guess we're getting used to this whole mating thing."

Lane grinned. "Believe me, when Jacqueline and I mated, things became both a little bit easier, and harder. You'll find your way."

"I forget that you and Jacqueline are mated. It's odd that you both have titles," Cruz stated, his voice a growl.

I shrugged. "We're the Centrals. We do things our own way."

Lane grinned at me as Cruz just snorted. "That used to be our thing with the Aspens. Now we're just a little weirder."

"And I'm part of both somehow," Adalyn said. "At least in my heart."

"And it's good you have that. You shouldn't ignore your past connections," Lane said pointedly, and I nodded tightly.

"Of course. I would never begrudge you that fact." I leaned forward, kissing the clean part of Adalyn's face.

"Now, did the bomb hit the truck?"

I hated bringing that up, hated hurting her. But we needed to know.

"It did, hit the underside and I landed on my side. It hurt like a bitch. But somehow I survived. They had to have known exactly what they were doing. He called me the Alpha bitch," Adalyn growled, the tension radiating from her pushing at my own wolf.

"So he wanted you specifically," Cruz asked.

"I think in retaliation for his own mate."

"And if he couldn't get Skye, then he would come for you," I said slowly, my eyes glowing gold.

Adalyn moved to put her hand on my chest, and it soothed me instantly. It was odd because Adalyn never soothed me. She always sent me over the edge or made my wolf growl. It was just how we were to one another. But now? Because of that bond? Things were different. And I could barely hold it all in.

Cruz looked between us and nodded tightly. "I'll go tell Chase everything. That way you guys have some time to breathe. I'm glad you're okay, pipsqueak," Cruz said as he winked. And I could tell he was doing his best to make sure that we knew that Cruz didn't have any intention to get close to Adalyn just then.

When she rolled her eyes and flipped him off, my gut told me that they were like brother and sister, even if I wanted to growl at his proximity. Cruz didn't lean forward or anything to say goodbye like a normal wolf would, instead he gave us a two-finger salute and left, as Lane looked between the three of us. "Okay. I'm almost done healing. You're going to be sore for a couple of days, but you and the baby are fine. Don't worry. Everything's fine."

Lane went back to work on something, and I froze, trying to understand exactly what she had just said. "I'm going to have to have you repeat that, Lane."

Lane's eyes widened. "I waited to say anything until Cruz was gone, because you hadn't announced it yet. But the Alpha and mates always know first. You can't tell?" Lane backed up a step, her gaze lowering from the intense stare of my wolf. I hated to do that to her, but I couldn't control it just then. Not when I could barely breathe.

"I'm going to need you to check again. Because you're saying that my mate is pregnant, and I'm a little confused."

"Yes, let's check again. Because shouldn't I be able to tell?" Adalyn asked, her voice high-pitched.

Nico just stood there, his mouth opening and closing as if he were a guppy.

Lane held out her hands. "I'm sorry. I honestly thought you knew, Alpha. You *should* have. You always know. The mates always know. Then the Alpha. Then me." Tears filled her eyes as she held out her hands. "And I haven't slept in like four days. I hadn't meant to say that out loud. I just... One second." She closed her eyes as she put her hand on Adalyn's stomach. I felt it then. That tiny spark. The bond that would one day come.

I looked at Adalyn and at Nico, and nearly fell to the floor.

"Oh my goddess," Adalyn whispered as Lane stepped back and wrung her hands in front of her. "I'm so sorry for just blurting it out like that. You know I don't normally do things like that."

I held up my hand and nodded. "I know. You didn't do anything wrong, Lane. You acted as you would have any other time. In the privacy of mates and their Healer you did exactly right. I just, that isn't what we expected."

"I suppose the moon goddess has plans for you three. Or perhaps four. Congratulations Alphas. I'll leave you be. But first, Adalyn? Rest. You need to rest. And then you can deal with everything else. I'll be here for the thick of it.

All of it. Just rest." Then she left, and I looked at my mates, confused.

"We're only *just* mated," Adalyn sputtered. "How on earth did this happen so quickly?"

I swallowed hard, feeling as though I were walking through jelly. "I don't understand."

"It's yours. You know that, right? One of yours. Biologically, even though emotionally it'll be both of yours. I haven't had sex in over two years—which is ridiculous considering the fact that I'm a dominant wolf and I need touch—but I haven't. I promise you, I haven't. The baby is yours."

I cursed under my breath and then leaned forward, cupping her face. Nico was at my side in an instant. "Of course, the baby's ours. I'm sorry for making you think any other way. I just needed a moment to breathe."

"You need a moment to breathe? There's something growing inside of me right now. What the hell just happened?"

Nico let out a sharp laugh, and we stared at him. "Not only did the moon goddess mate for us, she decided to give us a child on probably the first try. I can't even comprehend everything."

"I don't know what to do. I'm just now getting used to the fact that I have mates. That I have a new Pack. I wanted time to get used to this. I wanted a safe place to be a mother. I want to be a mother one day. Though when the first potential rejected me, I thought it would never happen. I'm not ready for this, boys. I'm really not. I'm not ready to be a mother. Or to have to protect this baby from demons and vampires who want them to die. Let alone the humans and witches who might not want us around because we're not handling the vampires like we should. I'm not ready for this."

Adalyn was voicing all of my concerns, but the only thing I could do was cup her face and press my forehead to hers.

"You are the strongest woman I know. You always have been. You are not alone in this. You have two mates to stand with you. I wasn't ready for this either. I'm still trying to get a handle on how to protect our Pack. Let alone two mates. And you were fucking hurt so I'm damn well not doing a good enough job in the goddess's eyes, am I?"

She pulled away as Nico stepped between us.

"You don't get to blame yourself for Adalyn getting hurt, just like I don't. Because maybe if I had been fast enough she wouldn't have been hurt at all."

"Both of you, stop it. We don't have time for you to blame yourselves for something that was the vampire's fault. But we have to stop Valac. I am not having this baby and looking into this new world and being scared out of my wits because that fucking vampire's out there wanting to take control of us. Fuck him. Oh my goddess. I'm going to have to stop cussing. When do I stop training? Or when can I not be out on the field? I'm not ready for this. I thought Skye or Audrey would be the first one with a baby. It wasn't supposed to be me." She put her hands over her mouth, tears sliding down her cheeks, and I leaned forward, holding her close. Nico wrapped his arms around both of us, and we stood there.

"I'm so scared to be happy," she whispered, and I nodded, crushing relief and worry filling me at once.

"I don't know how to be happy. But I thought maybe the two of you could show me."

Nico looked between us. "Well I'll damn well do my best to show you. Because I know happiness. And I know that I can find it with you two. And whatever obstacles we face."

"I want this baby," Adalyn whispered, as she looked between the two of us. My wolf preened, even as confusion set in. "I want this baby," she repeated. "But I want to make sure that we're safe first. Because if the moon goddess has a plan for us, then we need to figure it out. I'm not going to stand on the sidelines while our fate is decided for us. But I'm damn well not going to let this baby or our Pack get hurt because I'm mired in untruths and uncertainty."

I smiled then, I couldn't help it.

"Why are you smiling right now? Our lives are being thrown for loop after loop." She sounded so flabbergasted that I just smiled harder.

"Because no matter what happens, we fight for each other. What more do we need?"

Tears filled her eyes again, and I really had never seen Adalyn cry so much. That's how I knew something had changed. Not just along the mating bond, but in our lives forever.

I kissed each of my mates and held them close. I knew that everything had changed. Altered irrevocably.

I'd always had something to fight for, someone to fight for.

Now I had the world to fight for.

And I wasn't going to lose.

TWELVE

Adalyn

"Where do you want this, Jacqueline?" I asked, holding up the box of clothes. Jacqueline looked over her shoulder, narrowed her eyes, and gestured towards another pile. "Over there works. Thank you, Adalyn."

I smiled and hefted the box towards the other stack.

We were working on setting up a clothing and food drive for a small town that had been flooded in the last storm. Even though a lot of our den was rebuilding after the same flood, at least those who lived outside of the den proper, we were doing our best to help others.

Nico and Cole were over there now, helping to literally rebuild homes. I would have gone with them, but they had both growled at me for trying to help lift anything. Little did they know I'd be doing lifting here. But Jacqueline and I weren't going to tell them. The Heir of the Central Pack might be loyal to our Alpha, but she was a woman first and wasn't about to let the boys push me down into a nice little bubble-wrapped home.

"Okay, we're almost done here if you want to head over to the other den."

I looked up at her and smiled. "I don't have to. I can work a little bit longer."

Jacqueline shook her head. "No, you already had plans to work on the antidote with Dara and the others. That's more important than helping me lift a few boxes."

I scowled. "Everything that we're doing is important."

"I know you can handle this as well as things at the other den, but it's okay that you have to work over there. The Aspens have been at the forefront of ensuring that our Packs are safe. At least from this current threat. And you were and are an integral part of that. I'm not particularly jealous that you're spending time with your friends in another den. You're also helping here as much as you can. You're being a good Alpha's mate, Adalyn. A great one. You don't have to feel conflicted that your loyalties are in more than one place. If we ever went to war with the Aspens that would be different, but we won't. The four of us under this alliance are becoming one large Pack with four Alphas. We're becoming stronger than I ever thought possible. Especially with how I grew up."

I swallowed hard, surprised she was speaking about this. Jacqueline was private. So private that I'd barely said more than a word or two to her because she was focused on keeping the Pack safe and growing in its health rather than letting me know who she was beyond her title.

"I know you grew up with Cole. Outside the Pack structure."

"He and his sister Dawn were some of my best friends. Douglas protected us."

Douglas was now the Beta of the Pack. He was an older wolf and a good man.

"I don't think Douglas ever thought he'd get a title. But why wouldn't he? He protected us when we didn't have anything. I was just a kid, and there he was, growling at anything that came too close. And as soon as Cole was strong enough, he protected us as well. It wasn't a surprise to me when he became Alpha. Even if I think it surprised him."

I tilted my head and nodded. "That's how I feel. Like he doesn't think he knows what he's doing. But then again, Chase was the same way." I wasn't speaking untruths or secrets here. It was fairly evident to me and an Heir in Jacqueline's position that the two youngest Alphas felt as if they were thrown into this new world, because they had been.

"No matter what, we're going to find a way to stop Valac and the others. And whatever else comes after him. Because while I'm still new to this whole Central Alpha's mate thing, I'm not new to being a warrior. I'm a soldier. I'm a fighter. And I protect what's mine."

Jacqueline grinned. "I like that. However, how much longer are the boys going to let you fight in your current state?"

I frowned at her. "We're not talking about that current state," I mumbled.

Jacqueline could tell right away because of her connection to the Pack. But it was still far too early to let anyone else know. At least outside of my inner circle.

Wolves would soon be able to scent it, and there would be no hiding. But it had only been a few weeks. A few weeks of me somehow being a mate, living in a new den, fighting a war, and being pregnant.

It didn't make any sense. How could I be pregnant so quickly? I trusted the moon goddess, but I was really tired of her forcing these changes on me.

I put my hand over my stomach and let out a breath. "I'm still figuring this whole thing out."

"Are you nauseous yet?"

I shook my head. "No, I think it's too early for that. But what do I know? I've never been pregnant."

"You should talk with some of the maternals. I'm sure they could lead you down the path of motherhood. So could my mate."

She grinned as she said it, and I winced. "I'm so not ready for that. I'm so not ready for any of this."

"You will be," Jacqueline whispered, sobering up.

"Because you're Adalyn. You're a force. I've known of you my entire life."

"Way to make me sound like an elder," I said with a grin.

One problem with long-lived wolves was that I was indeed far older than most of the people in the Central Pack, even though they didn't always feel like it. They had gone through their own war, just like I had with the Aspens. Sometimes it was battles lived through rather than years lived that created a sense of age.

"It's true. We've all heard of you. The warrior who stood by Audrey's side and tried to fight for what was right. The warrior who deserved every accolade she ever got. You're training us to be stronger, emotionally and physically. And you were doing so even before you were mated. When you were just a visitor flirting with Cole and Nico."

"No one was supposed to notice I was flirting," I mumbled, and Jacqueline rolled her eyes.

"It's true though. All that fighting and growling with each other. We knew it was a matter of time before you tumbled into bed with him. The fact that you're mated is just perfect."

"I thought I was being sneaky, at least with those types of emotions."

"You weren't. But thank you for trying. As for what's coming next? The Alpha triad is about to have a child. It's a big thing. And when you're ready to celebrate we'll be here for you and maybe it'll finally kick me and Lane into gear about having a child of our own."

My eyes widened. "You're really thinking of it?"

"We've been talking. Deciding who would carry first. I think we're going to have to flip a coin for that."

I laughed. "Let's see how I do when I'm out waddling."

"That's what we're thinking. And, of course, we'll need a sperm donor."

I growled, my wolf pushing forward, even though I knew I was being ridiculous.

Jacqueline threw up her hands. "I am not about to ask two newly mated wolves to do it. Oh my word. Especially not my Alpha."

I held up my hands. "I'm sorry. I don't know what I was thinking."

"You're thinking like a newly married dominant wolf. It's okay. I don't blame you for getting territorial. Especially because you're a pregnant dominant wolf."

"I hate feeling out of control."

"It's going to get worse with all those hormones."

"Thank you for that, I'm so glad to know that I have someone to lean on when things get insane." I rolled my eyes and she tossed a bottle of water at me.

"Go see the Aspens. They need you. And we need you. Good thing you're strong enough to be with us both."

I leaned forward and hugged her, surprising her. The Heir to the Central Pack stiffened for a moment, before she wrapped her arms around me and hugged me tight.

"I'll be back soon."

"Sounds good. And you know you're not going alone right?" she asked with a growl, and I rolled my eyes.

"Of course not. I know better."

She narrowed her eyes at me, then nodded, and I made my way to my vehicle, two soldiers with me.

"Ready to go?" I asked, and both of them nodded, one sitting next to me, the other in the back seat.

"Thanks for not fighting us on this. Because I really don't want to deal with growly Alphas," Robert said.

Mercedes grinned at me from the back, and I just shook my head and made my way to the Aspens.

"Thank you for not fighting with me about who was driving."

"We can take turns," Mercedes said. "At least for shotgun."

I laughed. I was doing my best to deal with the growly Alpha. He didn't want me to drive alone, and honestly I didn't blame him right now. Especially when it looked like the mates of Alphas were targeted. But that meant Nico and Cole were no longer allowed to go by themselves either. Because fuck that. I might be pregnant, but I wasn't weak.

And dear goddess, I was going to throw up just thinking about it. No wait, that was something more. I pulled over to the side of the road, both wolves on alert, threw myself out of the car, and threw up right on the side of the road.

Another car passed, and since we were in the neutral area where humans and witches went, they didn't stop to look at us.

Mercedes got out of the car and handed me a paper towel and a bottle of water.

"Congratulations," he whispered.

I flipped him off. "I'm not ready to tell everyone."

"Your scent's changed, Adalyn. Plus, with the vomiting? I don't think you're going to be able to hold back any longer. Tell those you want to. Because the rest of us are going to figure it out."

I wiped my mouth and sighed.

"Why does everything feel like it's running out of control?"

"Because we're in the middle of a war. It's always going to feel like that."

With that pronouncement, I got back in the car and let Mercedes drive. Mostly because I was still nauseous, and I wasn't sure I could deal with it and drive.

Some dominant wolf I was.

We pulled into the Aspen Den and I held back a wince at the ward sensation against my skin. The two soldiers next to me did the same, and while it was sad to think that my former home felt different, the fact that I knew the Aspens were being protected overrode everything else. Nothing else mattered.

"We're off to go train with Cassius and Cruz and the others. You'll let us know if you need us?" Mercedes asked and I nodded.

"Go have fun. I'm going to go play with magic."

"Be safe, Adalyn," Robert growled, before he left with Mercedes, and I shook my head.

"Oh, you're here. Are you ready to go?" Lily asked as she smiled up at me.

I held out my arms and the young witch held me close.

"I'm glad you're here. Audrey and Skye are on patrol, and most of the other wolves are out working or helping clean up after that flood."

I nodded. "I was helping as well, and my mates are there now."

Lily beamed at me. "Look at you, sounding all proud like a peacock."

"I can't help it. I'm mated. With two very handsome men," I teased.

There was just something about Lily, she made me smile and remember that I did have good things in my life, even if it felt like sometimes that everything was out of my control.

I walked into Dara's home where we were working on our magical cure, and the death harvester witch looked up at me and grinned.

"You're here. I thought you were going to be spending more time in bed with certain Alphas."

I flipped her off, then went around the worktable and pulled her in to hug her tight.

"You're looking better, did you get some sleep?" I asked.

"Both Cruz and Steele forced her into it," Wren said as she walked inside.

I hugged the Healer, who froze and glared up at me.

"Were you not going to tell me?" she asked, her voice high-pitched.

I blinked, and then remembered that of course the Healer would know.

"Can nobody just let me tell them? Everybody's just finding out on their own."

Dara and Lily looked at each other, then us, before they both put their hands over their mouths and squealed.

I put my hands over my ears at the sound and then laughed as all three women bounced around me, hugging me close.

"I cannot believe it. Those boys were fast," Dara said with a wink. Then she froze. "Is it okay if I touch you? I swear I may be a death witch, but I don't bring death like that. I'm not going to harm you or your child."

I stared at one of my closest friends. "Of course you're not. Why would you ever think that?"

Dara's gaze darted from mine, and I looked at Wren.

"Another witch wouldn't let Dara come to the coven meeting because one of the other witches is pregnant. At least, that's the excuse that they used."

My wolf rose to the surface and my eyes glowed gold.

"Who do I have to burn?" I asked, and Dara burst out in laughter.

"I like how you go straight to burning. Not you know, clawing or gutting. But burning. It's quite nice and different."

"I'm a pregnant mated wolf. I need to change things up."

"I cannot believe it. Not only an Alpha triad but a baby too? When you change things, you go full force," Lily said with a laugh.

"Apparently. Now, I really want to focus on something else for a second. Only because I'm starting to freak out."

"I don't blame you," Wren said as she squeezed my hand. "I'll talk with Lane and make sure she has all your medical records. Now you're going to have at least two Healers on you."

I rolled my eyes. "Considering Nico's mother is also a Healer, I'm going to be bombarded with them."

Dara's eyes widened. "I forgot about that. Oh, you're going to have every Healer ever watching out for you. You are very blessed."

"Blessed is one word for it," I teased, and sat down on the stool next to Wren and stared at the cauldron.

"Okay, so we are trying to find an antidote to the black magic dust or whatever it's called that pulls magic from wolves and cuts into us like shards."

"Yes," Dara said with a growl of her own. "We're on try number four hundred, it seems."

"Only number eighty-seven," Wren mumbled as she took notes.

I winced at that and knew that this still might not work. There were many other magics that the vampires were using, and we didn't know where they came from. I had a feeling that had to do with the demon that created them rather than the vampires themselves. We knew that the demon created vampires, and vampires themselves could create hybrids. That was how they created their own versions—by biting and draining shifters. But hybrids weren't stable. At least as far as we knew. Hybrids didn't have the strength and ability to think for themselves and usually imploded if we didn't take them out first. Vampires took months to gain control of themselves from homicidal monsters who were in turn controlled by other vampires.

But all of that was the vampire problem, not part of the magic problem. They created their own personal wards, something that only Dara and a few others could even break, as well as those bombs. Some of the bombs were just magic that could push out and create destruction. But some of them held those black shards and dust that sank into a shifter and leeched out their magic. It had even forced a shifter back into human form without their control.

And as a shifter who prided myself on control because

that was how I functioned, that was scary and something that could not be tolerated.

So that was the one phase we were focusing on now. Just to find an antidote to whatever tried to control our own magic.

We would find an antidote and a magic that could go against it without going to demon or dark magic.

We had to.

Only, we didn't have the coven's backing on this. And I knew that annoyed Dara to no end. It was dejecting as hell. Because the coven only wanted to focus on their own magics and those who were of *pure* blood. Those of elemental blood. So they kicked out everybody that was with Packs or had magic they didn't like.

And they wouldn't focus on the vampire problem. They were too focused on another problem of theirs, and I had no idea what it was.

Right then, the only thing that I could focus on was this.

"What do you need from me?"

"Your blood," Dara blurted out, and I blinked and looked at the rest of them.

"Excuse me?"

"We have blood from Skye and Brynn, as well as Melanie," mentioning the three Alphas' mates.

"What do you need from me?"

"Your blood, of course. If the vampires can use their top magic against us to pull out our own connection to our wolves and the moon goddess, we're going to use a connection that they don't have. Love and mating and the fierceness of those in power. Alpha blood didn't work. But what of those connected by magic and comfort? There's a reason that all of our Alphas are now mated."

"I thought it was just so we had power," I said, confused.

Dara nodded. "That could be it. I don't know, this just feels right. And I would have asked Nico, but the idea of four women appeals to me."

Lily snickered and Dara winced. "Now that sounds like too much work for me, but what I meant was four women in power, strength in their own ways—submissive, former human, soldiers, warriors, gamma. All of you are of a different strength and a different background and a different purpose. I would think that Nico would be good for this as well, but for some reason I think it needs to be the four women. So just a drop of your blood, and then we'll see if this works."

"And if it does? How much more will you need?"

Dara winked. "I'll get a pint if I need to."

"What about the baby? Will it hurt the baby?" I asked my eyes wide, as I put my hands over my stomach.

Wren moved forward and put her hand over mine. "Just a prick of blood. The magic won't hurt the baby. I can feel this in my bones."

Dara nodded. "I know it won't. I don't know anything

else for sure, but I know your baby is safe from this. And from my magic."

There was something pained in my friend's voice, and I knew if I walked away now, I would not only be walking away from a potential cure for this poison, but I would also be hurting one of my best friends. So I nodded and held out my hand.

"Okay. I'm ready."

Dara pricked it with a needle, a single drop of blood welling from the tip. She took it from my finger with a single sage stick, before adding it to the cauldron in front of us.

Dara held out her hands, and I slid mine into hers, Wren holding my other. Lily held Dara's other hand, and I listened to Dara hum, the magic around her whirling. I let out a breath, my own wolf rising up to the sound of magic.

Dara began to chant in a language I didn't understand and knew I would never, and when she opened her eyes, they were white, no iris, no pupil, just white, and the entire room lit up in an eerie green glow. And as if somebody had popped a balloon, the air fizzled out, and I sank into Wren's side, both of us out of breath.

I looked up at Lily, who held back tears. Dara grinned.

"I think it worked."

I shook my head. "How do you know?" I asked, wiping the sweat off my brow. I didn't hurt. If anything, I felt energized, but I was a little worried about how tired Dara looked and the fact that the darkness in her gaze seemed to intensify.

The witch leaned forward. "Look."

I stared at the center of the cauldron. I realized that she had put a glass vial of that vampire magic inside. I didn't know how she had found it or kept it, and I wasn't sure I wanted to know. But the antidote swirled around it, and as I watched, those black magic spells disappeared. I blinked up at my friends and grinned.

"It worked."

"We have an antidote to one thing. To one thing, but that's so much more than we had," Dara said as she stood up. She looked at us then and then fell, her knees crumpling.

I reached for her as the door slammed open.

My mates were there, as were Chase and Cruz.

Cole and Nico came to my side, holding me close as I tried to pull away to look at my friend. But Wren was at Dara's side as Cruz held her close and growled at her. He shook her roughly, and I scowled.

"Cruz."

"No. Snap out of it, Dara. Wake up."

His growled order shocked me, but Dara opened her eyes and smiled.

"It worked, Grumpy Pants."

"You're a fucking menace," he growled, and then he made sure Wren was holding her, Chase at her side, and left the room.

Bewildered, I looked at everyone else, who shook their heads and stared at Dara.

"We have an antidote to the dark magic. We can save the wolves."

Everyone spoke at once while my mates held me close, and I knew we had done something great.

I just hoped it was enough.

Valac

THE VAMPIRES SCATTERED AS VALAC THREW THE nearest object towards the glass doors. The fact that it happened to be an antique chair that he had bought for Sunny a decade ago didn't matter. It wasn't as if she could ever sit on it again.

They had joked about it, because the spindles on the chair were made of the perfect wood to make stakes out of. If one could kill a vampire by impaling them on a wooden stake. Of course, taking out the heart like that could do it. Not that he would tell the shifters or humans about that.

So far the only ways they knew to kill vampires were to rip off their heads or to bleed them dry. The normal

ways you would kill a human or shifter, except for the fact
that vampires were far superior and could take a tougher
beating.

And yet none of that mattered.

Because the wolves had taken their little bitch queen
back.

He had failed.

No, his men had failed. The ones who had fallen and
were dead already didn't matter. But the ones that had fled
before he had?

They would be punished. They would all be
punished.

"I'm quite tired of your temper tantrums."

The deep voice behind Valac made him stiffen. He
rolled his shoulders back and tried to remember how to be
the suave, sophisticated general he had been for so long.
He and Sunny had thrived in power underneath his
master's rule. And yet, and yet.

Valac turned towards his master, his chin raised.

"Malphas. Master. You are here. I was unaware you
were coming and I am sorry that the place isn't up to its
usual opulence for you."

Malphas waved his hand, as if the shattered glass and
remains of the former dining room scattered among the
floor were nothing. Neither were the corpses of the three
humans Valac had drained on his way back. He had
needed their energy, their life's blood. That damned
Alpha had nearly gutted him, not that he would let anyone

know that. He had only survived thanks to the magics he held. The magics that took the lives of multiple humans to balance.

He was exhausted. Not that he would let anyone know that, either.

But using so much magic in such a short time took a lot out of him. His priestesses and priests were working their hardest to ensure they had their bombs ready. But as of now, the wolves were not losing, nor were they winning. They were at a stalemate, and Valac could not have that.

"As I said, I'm tired of your temper tantrums. The Aspen Alpha is still alive. And I would like to know why."

Valac raised his chin though he didn't meet Malphas' gaze. It was hard to meet a demon's gaze and live. That was something the others had learned the hard way long ago.

"We are working on it, Master. It will happen soon."

He waved Valac off. "Don't lie to me. I'm tired of lies. You were my most glorious general. One of the first I had made in my image. And yet here you are, bleeding again from a wound that a wolf made."

Valac looked down at his stomach and held back a grimace. A single line of blood slid down his shirt, the wound having opened after he threw the chair.

"No bother. It will heal soon. You have given me great power, Master."

"I have. Because I am powerful. I am the one who

gives you that power, and yet Chase and the other Aspens still live."

"Because they are cunning and using sacrifice through their weakness. We will not allow that to happen."

"Then why have you turned your attention to the Centrals? They are nothing. A worthless Pack that my predecessor thought he could wield. He lost and did nothing with them. Now they're just shadows of who they once were. No one to concern ourselves with."

Valac nodded, remembering the story of the first demon and his pact with the Centrals. That Pack had nearly been decimated, the new one only forming recently.

"It was an opportune moment to find that queen. As there are two mates, it would have been a striking blow to take her."

"And yet you did not. And if what my sources tell me are true, by not taking her now, you have just ensured their legacy for far beyond this moment."

Valac stiffened. "What sources?"

Valac knew of one, one that would taint that Pack until the end of their days. But they didn't know it, and Valac would not be the one to voice it. For if he did, the walls could have ears and this long con would never work.

"You don't need to know my sources. You don't need to know my plans beyond what I tell you. Find a weakness. Exploit it. Or I will replace you. It would pain me to do so, Valac. For you and Sunny were my favorites. But she is gone, and your vengeance is standing in the way of our power. My power. And I will not allow this to happen."

Malphas moved forward and slowly trailed his claw along Valac's jaw. Valac did his best not to shudder, to show his revulsion or fear.

Because if he did, Malphas would see it as pure weakness and end Valac before he could take his next breath.

Malphas was a demon from Hell, and held the power.

But Valac would not fail.

He couldn't.

"If I take out the Centrals, it will be their weakening within this new alliance. The Aspens are so worried about their own strength and their wards because of past attacks, they are not prepared for us. They would not be prepared for us to take the Centrals out as well. And the Aspen queen's best friend is now the Central queen. We could use this to our advantage."

Malphas studied Valac's face, a cruel smile on his lips. "The Centrals are weak. We eliminate them from the board quickly and then we can focus on the ones that I want. That's a good idea, Valac. I don't need the other demons' taint on my legacy. Take out the Centrals, and then we will focus on what we need to. The Aspens. Because they hold the power that we need. And I want it."

Malphas turned and left, not waiting for an answer.

Valac was unsure he could give it to him.

Because now he had a true calling. To take out the

Central Pack, to surprise the alliance and have them bleed.

And once the Central Pack Alpha was grieving for his dead mates, for his dead Pack members, they could focus on the true enemy.

The Aspens.

And the legacy they seemed to have forgotten.

CHAPTER
FOURTEEN

Nico

THE GROUND BENEATH MY PAWS SHOOK AS I RAN, letting the magic within my veins pulse. I jumped over a grouping of roots, remembering when I had tripped and fallen flat on my face. My brother had laughed, that wheezy laugh that only wolves could do in shifter form, and had rolled on the ground, his legs kicking in the air.

It had been good to see my brother Conner laugh like that, his whole body shaking. Because Conner hadn't laughed and smiled like that in a while. Now he was mated, happy, and heading towards a future that meant something more than fear. But at that time when I had been so focused on seeing how fast I could go, my tripping had at least released some pressure.

I jumped off a large boulder and kept moving, keeping my attention on the world around me, as well as what was below me.

The magic within the earth connected to the bonds that made me wolf and part witch. That in turn increased my speed. But even as I did that I needed to focus on what was around me.

I was on patrol outside of my new den, Douglas my patrol partner. He wasn't moving as fast as I was, but the older wolf was all brawn and brain wrapped up into one.

When I made it to the edge of our territory, I circled back, letting Douglas come to my side. He pressed his nose against my flank, and I huffed out a breath, as we continued to move. Neither one of us had scented intruders, the magic covering the wards doing what they were supposed to. That also meant that we couldn't scent vampires around. With the antidote that the Aspens and Adalyn had worked out, it gave all of us on patrol a sense of hope. But that wasn't the only thing. Because the shifters would be able to survive an attack if they got the antidote to them in time, their magic would survive as well. However, the vampires still had that darkness that led to stronger bombs.

Plus, vampires were just as strong as shifters, which was weird to think. Something that hadn't been heard of. All of my life I had always thought that it was shifters with the most strength. Yes, humans and their weapons and intelligence had hurt us in the past, and so had demons, but the fact that this new enemy was just as strong if not stronger worried me.

Douglas tilted his head at me and studied my face, and I nodded, knowing that we needed to move.

It was odd to think that he was asking me, considering he was the Beta for this Pack. While the Enforcer protected the den from outside forces, it was the Beta's role to check for inside threats. For malcontent, for needs that might not be said aloud.

I knew my uncle as Beta of the Redwoods had even done minor plumbing repairs and other things inside the den when we had been stuck inside the wards thanks to a war of our own. It wasn't like we could just hire a plumber to come in and fix the pipes on an old rundown building. We had to learn skills, and the Redwoods and Aspens and Talons I knew had plumbers within their den now. Wolves and humans that had learned the trade because they wanted to, and it was needed.

There was a whole engineering department, as well as the maternals that helped with the education and play for the children. The clinic might be headed by the Healer, but there were nurses and aides that didn't have the magical abilities that the Healer had, but were still qualified for what they did.

The Centrals were small enough however, that everybody had to become a jack-of-all-trades.

That was something I knew Cole was trying to change, to have people specialized in certain aspects. And that's where Douglas came in for now. Because Douglas had to see what the Pack needed that sometimes an Alpha couldn't.

Cole had to think about everything at once; the government, the humans, the witches, the vampires, and everything inside the Pack as well. He had to give a part of himself to every single person that came to him. Every single person that needed him. So that meant he needed to rely on his people to see what slipped through the cracks.

Douglas did that, as did the Enforcer, the Healer, and the Omega.

They each had their roles, and I was the Alpha's mate. I was support for him, and yet I was a higher rank than most somehow.

We made our way to our clothes and shifted, the change excruciating as always. It was a painful bliss that melded bones and skin and fur somehow into this human body. I shook off the sweat that came from the run and the shift and pulled on my pants and shoes, my shirt coming last.

I had learned from other soldiers that it was easier to fight shirtless than it was shoeless, so I always made sure that I had shoes on before I put on my shirt. At least while I was training or on patrol.

Douglas was slower to shift back, and it shocked me. Mostly because it hadn't always been the case.

I looked down at my hands, pulled in the magic within my body, and frowned. I was stronger than I had been before. And not only as shifter, but the magic within my veins.

"You're the Alpha's mate now. It unlocks the potential. You didn't steal Cole's powers, but now you have more access to what you should have had in the beginning. Because you are support, you are Alpha's mate, and your place in the hierarchy means that you have the strength allotted to you from your own power."

I frowned at the other man. "How did you know what I was thinking?"

"Because it startled me that you shifted so quickly. You've always been quick at everything, but that was new."

I winced. "Sometimes I feel like I'm still learning everything all at once, like a pup."

"The world is changing every day. Maybe that's what we're doing. Relearning. Being Cole's mate doesn't change who you are."

I barked out a laugh. "I thought that's what you just said."

There was a rustle behind me and I turned, on alert before the scent hit me.

Cruz flew out from the trees, his shirt in his hand, his body covered in sweat.

"Sorry, I was finishing my run out here and heard you, and I didn't want to startle you."

I looked at the Aspen Pack wolf and nodded. "I forgot you were meeting with Cole later today."

"I decided to run it since we could always use more guards on this flank. But I was listening to what you were saying."

"Of course you were, wolf," Douglas barked out with a laugh.

Cruz flashed a set of white teeth and I just rolled my eyes.

"Since you were eavesdropping, what do you want to say?"

"That the moon goddess may confound us sometimes, but I think she did you right here. You've always been strong, Nico, and not just in strength of limb and claw. But of heart."

I frowned. "I've never heard you speak so poetically."

He flipped me off as Douglas laughed outright.

"The Talon Pack Alpha's mate is submissive. She's always been and that won't change. But the strength of her heart is what proves that she was the perfect person for that Alpha. Adalyn is so dominant sometimes it hurts to be near her," Cruz added, and I nodded. "But that just means that her strength was needed for Cole. Yours is different."

"I'm not submissive. Not that there's anything wrong with being that," I added quickly.

"Of course not. Everybody is needed within the Pack, and their relative strengths and who they are as a wolf is needed as well. Without submissives, who do the dominants need to be strong for? Not just for themselves. At least that's what happens in a healthy Pack. You and Adalyn balance out Cole just like you balance out each other. I've liked this new person that you're becoming."

"I've never seen you so introspective before." I narrowed my eyes at Cruz. "Do you want to talk about it?"

Cruz just rolled his eyes. "No, thank you. I'm just fine on my own. Now, let's get back to the den, because I want to meet with Cole and get this over with."

"Be careful how you speak of our Alpha," Douglas warned, even though the wolf in his gaze seemed happy.

I just grinned, threw my arm around Cruz's neck, and pulled him down.

"Come on, I think I can take you now with all this power running through my veins," I teased.

At the word power, however, magic danced along my skin, and I staggered back, staring.

"Something's coming."

Cruz cursed under his breath, and we moved, our wolves at the forefront as we followed our senses towards wherever that magic came from.

Both Douglas and Cruz pulled out their phones, barking orders to their respective Packs. I let them do it, knowing that I was faster. I needed to be the one who did this.

At the first explosion, I got knocked back into Cruz, and we both rolled to the ground, landing on our feet again. Douglas was close behind, cursing.

"Another bomb? But that's an unpopulated area. What the fuck are the vampires thinking?"

"It smells of them, of their magic, so it has to be them. But what the hell? Did it go off early?"

"We still need to go over there, make sure nobody was camping or out for a run. It might be unpopulated, but that doesn't mean it's always empty."

We made our way there, as Douglas let out a string of curses.

"Damn it. What were they thinking? Right against that mountainside? They could have killed themselves."

I froze before I closed my eyes and drew on the magic within.

As Cruz and Douglas argued about fault lines and if the vampires accidentally set it off, I focused on the earth magic flooding through my veins, thanks to my mother.

I heard Cruz and Douglas continue to search, commenting that nobody seemed to be there, just the charred remains of a magical bomb that they called in.

But that's not what worried me.

Because deep within the mountainside was a fault line that I had noticed before. One that I always paid attention to because of where it stood outside of the Central Pack.

One that was connected to far more than just a single point. One that the vampires seemed to know about and had been very strategic about.

I opened my eyes. "Run!"

There must have been something in my voice because

the two men turned and stared at me, and that was when the ground moved.

I turned, knowing that they would follow me as I ran, the earth beneath our feet rolling in waves.

"Earthquake!" Douglas shouted as if it wasn't obvious. But perhaps we needed to make it clear, because earthquakes like this didn't happen here often, if ever. No, this was magical in nature, stress triggered by magic that had no business being here.

"Get to the den. We're right behind you," Cruz called out as I left them behind, knowing that they would help each other make it. But I needed to get to the den. The magic within me pushed, clawing at my skin just like my wolf would have.

I didn't use the magic to run faster, not beside the inherent way that I moved. Because I needed to use that magic for something else.

I looked up at the mountain beside the den, and knew I had this magic for a reason.

It was as if everything clicked, and this was why I was here.

Because there were no other witches that could do this. I was the only one.

The lead sentry outside of the den pointed behind me, and I nodded tightly.

"Get everyone to the other side of the den. Now!" I ordered.

His eyes were wide, his wolf in his gaze, and as I

barked out the order again he moved, and I turned on my heel, facing what was coming at me.

The earth was no longer moving from the small quake. No longer moving from the bomb that had set it off.

The earthquake had set off a series of events that I had been dreading ever since I knew what lay beneath the surface.

The land moved, rocks and dirt and soil and trees pummeled down the mountain, coming straight towards the Central den.

There was no one to stop this, it would blanket the den, and the ward wouldn't block it. The ward stopped humans and other shifters and demons and vampires from getting in.

It did not stop the land or snow or other elements.

It would not stop the landslide currently shifting towards the den.

I had to find a way to stop it, even if it killed me. So I shoved off my shoes, dug my toes into the soil, and closed my eyes. I held out my hands and connected to the earth that made me a witch, that made me my mother's son.

"Dear goddess, *help*."

I knew she wouldn't be able to help, but I needed to say something. Needed to do something.

I pulled at the magic within me, that small spark that set me aside from other shifters but didn't make me a full witch.

186

But there was something there, something always there.

My energy burned within me, a flash of fire that turned to stone. I sucked in a breath and hoped to hell this didn't kill me. Because I was deeply afraid if the landslide didn't kill me, the magic would.

I pressed my palms out, shoved them forward, and prayed to the goddess.

A wall of earth and dirt shot up before me and moved forward as if there were two waves competing against one another. A wave of destruction and a wave of my own power. I kept my hands up, sweat pouring down my temples as my entire body shook, as the magic and strength within me began to drain.

But people were screaming, and I knew I wouldn't be able to save them all, wouldn't be able to stop everything, but I would stop as much as I could. I knew that now. I knew this was why I was here.

So I pushed out, everything within me breaking, shaking. It sounded like two giants slammed into each other, echoing off the land in every direction, and I fell to my knees, blood seeping out of my nose, sweat pouring down my body.

The landslide from the earthquake continued to move, but slower, and at least a fifth of the size it had been. It wouldn't hit the den completely, just part of it, and hopefully everyone would get out in time. It was moving slower. There was still a chance.

But I couldn't move, couldn't get out of the way. I fell to my knees, my energy drained, my magic spent, and slammed into the ground headfirst, exhausted, my eyes closing.

But then a familiar scent covered me, my Alpha, my mate, and Adalyn was there too.

I would growl at her later for daring to get in the way, to put herself and the baby in danger. But I would have to survive in order to make that happen.

The scent of my mates enveloped me.

Then there were murmurs, and other sounds that I couldn't quite figure out.

The impact never came.

The earth didn't come, and so I let my mates hold me.

FIFTEEN

Cole

"Get Nico to Lane," I ordered Douglas as he and Cruz came out of the forest, covered in dust and dirt but seeming otherwise no worse for wear.

"You might not be my wolf, but thank you," I said to Cruz, knowing the other wolf had helped pull in a couple of the wolf teams who had been playing near the edge of where the disaster occurred.

"Of course, they're pups. I'll help with Nico."

I nodded tightly, grateful for the other man. I trusted him. Which was weird considering he wasn't my Pack, but I trusted him with my mate. So, as he and Douglas took

Nico over to where Lane had set up triage for those who had been hurt, I turned to Adalyn.

Her eyes were gold. "He's okay. I feel him along the bonds. He just overdid it."

I nodded tightly, studied her face. "You threw yourself on top of him when the wall came. I'm trying not to be angry for that, but you could have fucking hurt yourself and the baby."

"It had stopped by the time I did. And both of my mates were in the line of fire. Of course, I was going to be there to protect you."

"You could have been hurt," I snapped.

She shook her head. "We're in the middle of a war, Alpha. I can always be hurt. I'm trying to be good, but you need to understand that things aren't easy. Okay? I can't stay home in cotton wool."

"I want to keep you safe." Alive. "But why do you have to constantly throw yourself in the middle of danger?"

"Because I'm your mate. And that is why we became friends to begin with. Because we always throw ourselves in danger. Do you not remember the bomb that nearly killed us both? The one where they had to piece you back together again? I remember that. And what did we do? We threw ourselves on top of Lily to protect her. I'm not sure why you're so surprised that I'll do it now. Nico is awake. He'll be fine. You are so worried, and you can't yell at him so you're yelling at me. I'm only going to let you do that once. And then I'm done."

"Adalyn—" I began, but she held up her hand.

"Do your thing. I'm going to check on Nico and then finish his patrol. Because that was just a warning. You know it was."

I wasn't so sure about that. It seemed a little too strategic. But I was going to investigate, along with my witches. I needed to call the coven and see if they would send help.

I was a little worried that they wouldn't.

She went off behind Cruz after leaving me a quick kiss on my cheek, and I held in a breath, trying not to growl.

"Alpha?" Jacqueline asked as she came to my side.

"What?" I snapped and sighed.

She raised a brow, but she didn't yell at me for my outburst. I would have yelled at me.

"The mayor is on the phone."

I rolled my eyes, and she snorted before she held out the phone, and I moved off to the side. We still had cleanup to do, and it looked as if Nico was the worst injury. But he would be fine. Everybody kept telling me that he would be fine. He'd just overdone it on the magic thing. But I had never seen anything like that before. His magic had been beautiful. So fucking strong, and I hadn't even known he had had it in him. I knew he was strong, but I didn't know it was like that.

I didn't know he had held that. And the whole Pack had seen it.

My Pack had respected him before, but now they would as more than just my mate. He had done something for the Pack, just like Adalyn had every time she protected this den.

My mates were finding their way around this den, and it meant the world.

I finally answered the phone, grateful I was out of hearing distance of the others.

"Mayor Tenant, this is Cole."

"Alpha Cole, we heard about the landslide outside of town. Are your people okay?"

Mayor Tenant was very much an Alpha in his own right. And it didn't fail to cross my mind that the other man put this disaster in perspective of where the human town was, and not the den lands. Very interesting. I would have thought that Tenant might have done it by accident, but no, he was very purposeful in his words. He was making sure that I knew exactly where we lay versus the humans. I wasn't ecstatic about that.

We didn't have the major city that the Talon Pack did, nor the Redwoods. We had a smaller town that was growing by leaps and bounds. However, there were very firm lines about whose territories were whose. But some of our people lived within that town. Many of my people did. And Tenant had to deal with that. Hence the strained relations.

"We are fine. It was a vampire bomb that caused the landslide."

I wasn't going to lie to him or keep secrets. Not when we needed to work together for the vampire problem.

Tenant was quiet for long enough that I was afraid that the connection had been lost. "Did you find those vampires?"

"No. From what it looks like, the vampires left the bomb there a while ago. Their scent had dissipated."

"And there's not some magical thing that you can use to keep them out?"

"Wards don't work like that, Mayor. You know that."

"So I keep hearing. What about the coven? Have you talked to them?" he asked, worry in his tone.

I held back a curse. "I'm going to be calling them right after I get off the phone with you. But no, this is not something that they do."

"Why not? All of you paranormal things—people, I'm sorry—should work together, shouldn't you? To protect us?"

There were many things wrong in his statement, but I knew Tenant was trying. He didn't mean to be an asshole. He was actually trying, which was more than I could say for some humans in power.

"We have different governments and powers. But in the past we have worked together to help one another. We are doing all in our power to stop the vampires from this guerrilla attack."

"And what about their endgame? Taking over the world seems like kind of a weird endgame."

"Not if you're a megalomaniac," I mumbled. Tenant snorted, and I was grateful that I seemed to have calmed him down a bit. Not that I was calm at all. "I'll speak with the other Alphas. My people will be safe. Keep yours safe as well. I'll talk with the covens to see if there's something we can do. But, until we find out exactly what the next steps are for the vampires, all we can do is make sure people understand that the vampires are out there."

"That's the problem, Alpha Cole. We do understand that. And we're the weaker ones here. The vampires are killing my people. They're coming through our town and taking them from their homes. We try to keep them safe, and I know your people are on guard to keep the humans safe as well, but it doesn't seem like we're strong enough. Shouldn't the shifters, humans, and witches together be enough to overpower the vampires?"

I wanted to say yes. I wanted to say of course. But I wasn't sure that was the case. Especially not when I wasn't sure the three factions were working together as they should. But that wasn't something I could say right then, not when I was still trying to find out answers.

The mayor hung up after a few more reassurances, but I knew we were just treading water at this point. Until we all pulled together against the vampires I didn't think we would be able to find an end to this.

We needed to stop Valac. And whoever his leader was.

And while I was thinking about all of this, all I wanted to do was go sit by Nico's bedside and make sure he was okay. It didn't matter that I could feel him along the bond. That I knew that Adalyn and Cruz were with him.

None of that mattered.

I couldn't focus on anything but Nico.

That reminded me of his magic though, and I knew what I needed to do next.

I pulled out my phone and dialed the one person I didn't want to.

Anastasia answered on the first try, and I was surprised. I wasn't sure she would.

The coven's second in command sounded airy on the phone, but I knew her words could cut like a knife.

"Cole. It's so good to hear from you. Should I say congratulations on your mating?"

"Anastasia," I growled out, trying to keep my voice as level as possible. It wasn't working. She always seemed to put me on edge, and not in a good way. She hadn't liked me before I was mated other than wanting to bed me, and it didn't matter that she was already mated. She wanted power, and her mate Henrik, the coven leader, seemed to give her that. But she wanted more.

But I was mated now and I was off limits. Though in my mind I always had been. Now I just had an actual excuse that wasn't simply "get the fuck away from me."

"To what do I owe this pleasure? And it is a pleasure, Alpha."

I ignored the taunt like I always had. "The vampires attacked again. We need a meeting. With the full council."

The full council would include members from each of the four Packs, some Alphas, and the Supreme Alphas. I missed the old coven with Amelia and Diana. But they were gone now, murdered. Some had said it was a natural death, but we knew it was murder. And we knew who had done it.

The change in the command structure of the coven was a little too swift for our liking. And we didn't like who was now on it. And who wasn't allowed to be part of it.

The fact that Nico wasn't even allowed to be near the coven anymore because he wasn't a witch in their eyes grated on me. But there wasn't anything I could do right then.

"I'm afraid the coven has been doing some restructuring. With these new threats, we must worry about our powers as witches. You are strong, Alpha," she said after a pause.

"You're going to abandon us?"

"Of course not. Of course not. We will get back to you soon, Alpha." She hung up before I could say anything, and it took everything for me not to crush my phone in my hand.

The vampire magic was increasing and Valac was insane. That much I knew. We had to get to him and who was controlling him. But that was the problem; we didn't know exactly who was in charge. Sunny was gone, their first general was gone. And Valac was the only one left we knew of. We were missing something big, and we needed the coven to work with us. Only they kept blowing us off and I knew one day that powder keg would blow.

I moved back towards the fray, knowing there was nothing else I could do to convince the coven to help for now, and I quickly summarized the call for Jacqueline. She growled but nodded, and I knew she would take care of letting people know.

For now, I went to my Pack, held them close, and let them know that I would be here no matter what. Even in the unknown.

"What Nico did? That was amazing. We're glad that he's one of us," a small submissive wolf said as I hugged her close. I kissed the top of her head as her Alpha, and she sighed into me.

"I'm very blessed to have him. We all are."

"Go see him, I know you want to. We'll clean up the mess. We've got you, Alpha."

Something shifted inside of me, just a moment of peace. This was what I had wanted. That happiness. And yet it felt as if things were sliding through my fingers even as I was trying to hold on.

I spoke to every person that wanted to speak to me, as well as a few who were a little more reluctant. But they needed their Alpha, and I needed to do what I could.

I made my way to the clinic and Lane came out, a smile on her face. A smile was good.

"He's awake and grumbly, and he wanted to make sure you were okay since you hadn't come to see him like Adalyn had."

Guilt hit me hard and Lane's eyes widened. "We were

just messing around. He knows what you are doing. We all do. He saw you when he woke up."

"I need to go to him."

"Of course you do, Cole. Now go. Don't make me sic the Omega on you."

I held up my hands. "Anything but that." I wasn't exactly teasing either. The Omega did their best to ease the emotional strain on each of their Pack members. Some people needed it. Some people enjoyed it. I wanted nothing to do with it.

That was probably something I would eventually need to deal with.

I made my way back inside and saw Nico sitting up.

"You should be lying the fuck down," I growled.

My mate widened his eyes at me.

"Hello to you too. I'm fine."

"You used too much magic." I pushed his shoulder and laid him back down on the bed.

He rolled his eyes at me but smiled softly. "Everyone's okay, though, right?"

"Because of you." My body shuddered, and I leaned down, pressing my lips to his. "I could have lost you."

"We could have lost everyone else. I'm glad that I figured out how to do that."

I froze and then glared at him. "Excuse me?"

"I don't do that type of magic, Cole. You know that. Don't get mad at me."

"I can get mad at you if I have to. What the fuck do you mean you 'figured out how to do that'?"

"I'm not a witch. I'm a wolf. Trying to figure things out. I don't know why you're acting so surprised."

"Because my mate just said that he risked himself and didn't know if he'd actually make it out alive."

"You do that every day as Alpha. Don't growl at me."

"I can growl if I want to."

"Okay. Nico needs rest, and you need to go see your other mate because you're getting growly," Lane said as she walked inside. "I kind of like having two mates for you to deal with. That means you get out of my hair."

"Don't start, Healer."

"I can do what I want to. Now go. You did everything that you could for your Pack. You gave them every part of you. Now go for a run or something because I need you out of here."

I knew she was teasing, but was probably being truthful. I kissed Nico hard on the mouth, glared at him, and my mate just smiled.

"I'll rest. And guess what, my parents are coming here soon anyway to check in on me. You know my mom, she'll want to understand the whole witch thing."

It didn't matter that Nico was a full-grown adult, and my age for that matter, the fact that his parents were coming made me nervous.

He waved me off and I was forcibly removed from the clinic's room, thanks to my Heir and Healer's mate.

She kicked me out, physically. I grumbled and made my way to where I scented Adalyn.

I kept going, grateful others were leaving me alone. They seemed to realize at least subconsciously that I needed a moment.

"Why are you growly?" Adalyn asked as I walked through the forest towards her. She looked over her shoulder at me, her gaze fierce.

"I felt you, you know. I don't think I like you out here. On watch where you could get hurt."

I must have been exhausted because I hadn't meant to say that out loud. And while part of me felt that was the truth, most of me didn't actually agree with that. I liked her being a soldier. I liked her doing what she could to protect the world.

"I'm pregnant. I'm not weak."

I turned to her then, my wolf rising to the surface. "I know you're not weak. There's nothing weak about you."

She snorted. "You say that, and then you get grumbly."

"You growled at me because I was out on patrol alone as the Alpha. I'm not quite sure you have a leg to stand on."

She put her hand on my chest and my wolf pushed forward, the heat between us startling.

"I will always worry about you, Cole. When we were just friends, and now that we're something more. I am having a baby. It's so fricking weird. I can't even comprehend that, and I'm trying to act normal, but nothing is normal about our mating or what we're doing. Nico could have died today. All of us could have. I feel like we're three steps behind, but all I want to do is just hold onto you guys and never let you go. It's selfish of me."

"You're not selfish. You're allowed to want a moment for yourself."

I pushed her hair back from her face and she smiled into my touch. "I've missed you, Alpha. Our training schedules have been opposite, and I've only had a few moments of you each night. The mating urge is still strong. My connection is still strong. And I miss you."

That's what I loved about Adalyn. She didn't hold back saying what she wanted. And right then she wanted me just as much as I wanted her. I looked around, inhaled deeply.

"We're off the trail. No one's around."

Her eyes went gold and she smiled.

"Okay. That's a line, but I'll take it."

I laughed, then slid my hands over her arms before leaning down and brushing my lips against hers.

"Let me have you, Adalyn."

"I'm glad that she chose you for me," Adalyn whispered, and my throat closed up for a moment before I let out a deep breath.

"I would have chosen you no matter what," I said honestly, and her eyes widened before I captured her lips with mine.

There were no more reasons to talk, not when this was

even more important. We needed this moment to ourselves. Because while we were three, we were also two. Just like she and Nico were two, and Nico and I were two. A poly relationship meant that we actually had to realize that it was more than just the three of us. It was the combination of all. So in this moment we would just be the two of us, and knew that Nico would be smiling, knowing exactly what we were doing, as he would feel it along the bond.

Because this was who we were, a true triad in every sense of the word.

I kissed her harder. She growled against me, and that was when my beautifully dominant wolf tugged at my shirt and clawed it off. I did the same to hers, knowing we were destroying each other's clothes, but it didn't matter. I let my claws out and slid down her jeans, ripping them from her body. She shoved me and I fell back, the ground soft beneath my back thanks to the disturbance in the soil, and then she was straddling me, both of us naked as we clawed at each other, nipping and sucking and licking. She tasted of strength and Adalyn, and I was falling more and more in love with my mate with each passing moment.

And not just because of her beauty, not because of her heart, but her strength and her will and everything that aggravated me.

I was falling for all of it.

So I kept kissing her, letting her kiss me, and when she

rocked along my cock, both of us flinched, letting out a shocked breath.

"Oh my, is that steel pipe for me?"

"I'm always hard for you, woman. It's hard to walk sometimes when you're around. I'm fucking bowlegged."

"How do you think I felt when I had to practically limp to training with the others that one day after both you and Nico took me hard from behind. I thought I was going to die. Mostly of embarrassment."

I reached up and nipped at a lip.

"You liked it."

"Of course I did. Because you're mine."

I groaned, then slid my hand between her legs, pressing my thumb along her clit as she shuddered.

"Crawl over me, ride my face, woman."

She laughed, but she did as she was told, and I licked her nipples as she crawled up me. She shuddered, and then her thighs were on my shoulders and she was over my face. She rocked her hips and I clamped my mouth down on her cunt, licking and sucking her sweet juices. She arched above me, and I watched as she cupped her breasts, tugging gently at her nipples.

I sucked in a breath as I moved, looking up at her.

"Are your nipples sensitive?" I whispered.

"So fucking sensitive."

I knew it was because of the pregnancy, and it was such a strange thing to think, that we were having a child, the three of us. But, right then, I just needed to be with my woman. So I licked and I ate at her, gorging myself on her taste. She came on my face, her whole body writhing, I kept licking and sucking until she crawled off me, practically curling into a ball with shivers.

I grinned, then rose to my knees, gripped her thighs, and pulled her back. Her claws dug into the soil as she tried to scramble away, but I just smacked her ass and pressed my cock to her back.

"Get ready for me."

"You're a damn machine. I think I'm still coming."

She shuddered as she said the words, and then I pistoned right into her in one thrust.

She froze, her cunt tight around my dick, but I kept moving, needing her, knowing she wanted this.

"Harder," she growled, and I grinned.

I had thought I'd been doing hard enough, but apparently not. I wrapped her hair around my fist, arched her back, and moved fast. I thrust into her, hard and fast and wet and everything I needed.

She came again, surprising me, which made my balls tighten, and I was ready to slide over the edge.

But I needed more, wanted more. So I pulled out of her, and rolled her onto her back, pressed her knees up to her shoulders, and slid down deeper, and deeper and deeper.

She clawed at my arms, leaving blood trails in her wake, my dominant female wolf who wanted everything.

I finally came, filling her, both of us growled and then

clamped our mouths onto each other, needing one another.

The heat died down, and my wolf howled.

My mate writhed beneath me.

She was mine. Always.

And I would fight the world to keep her safe.

SIXTEEN

Adalyn

THROUGHOUT MY LONG YEARS OF LIFE, I'VE WOKEN UP in more than a few unique situations. I've had lovers, loves, and heartaches. I've woken up under the moonlight, in rain, and under a meteor shower.

I've also woken up hungover to the end of the earth and feeling as if I'd thrown up sandpaper the night before.

But waking up to the feel of two strong men holding me as if they never wanted to let me go was something new. At least new in the past few weeks.

I was mated to not one but two men who would risk everything for the people they loved without a second thought. That should scare me because they were risking their lives and our future when they did so, but in the end, I'd do the same. And perhaps that was something else that brought us together.

The idea we would never give up who we were to be with one another.

It was odd to think that I was a mated woman, a wolf finding a new path. Considering I'd spent most of my life fighting with the path laid out in front of me, I honestly wasn't surprised that fate had taken this chaotic turn for my love life and future. After all, it wasn't as if I was good at listening to the fates before this.

And with the vampire attacks increasing with such frequency recently, I hadn't had too many moments with *both* of my men. We were usually running on patrols, dealing with Alpha things, or setting up Pack processes that would change our futures forever. Not to mention that both Nico and I were constantly at our former Packs, as we had responsibilities and family there as well.

A hand curved around my hip, another around my ass, and I grinned into Cole's neck. I sniffed at him, my wolf on alert.

"I enjoy waking up like this," I mumbled to both of them.

Nico squeezed my hip and bit down gently on my neck. If I was a cat, I would've purred.

"You're awake. Finally." Nico nibbled on my ear and I groaned, rocking between them.

In the days since the earthquake and landslide, Nico

had healed, and I would be forever grateful. I would never get the sight of him standing full force in front of a landslide of dirt and rock and everything else imaginable out of my mind. He had almost died, and I would've been powerless to stop it.

Cole let out a little growl, his wolf in his gaze. "You're thinking again. I don't like it when you think."

I rolled my eyes. "Oh, that's nice. You don't like your mate to think at all?" I asked, my voice a singsong.

Nico laughed behind me. "You're naked between two naked men. You should be thinking about us and our cocks. And your pussy of course."

I snorted. "Well, that's a vivid picture. However, the alarm is about to go off any minute now, and you, Cole darling, have a meeting with the Alphas. Including the Supreme Alphas. Max and Cheyenne just got back from traveling Europe. They don't really have time for us to canoodle this morning."

"I like the word canoodle. Nobody uses it anymore," Nico said with a sigh as he slid out of bed behind me. I was cold at the loss, but he helped me get out of bed before bending down and kissing my belly. We both froze, and I looked up at him.

"It's feeling real, isn't it?" I whispered, my hands going over my stomach.

I couldn't feel the baby. It was far too early for that. But there was a life growing inside of me. Something I hadn't expected to want so soon. I felt like we were just getting to know who we were together as mates. I knew these men. They were my friends. It wasn't as if we had to start from scratch, but other parts felt like we were starting over.

"It's going to be really real in a few months when you're all waddling and cute."

"I'm not going to waddle," I growled.

"Oh, you're so going to waddle."

"I'm going to like to see that," Cole said, his chest pressed out like a cock on a walk.

I rolled my eyes. "I swear, you both act as if sperm changes the world."

"It does," both men said in unison.

I snorted. "Oh stop. You need to go to the office and meet with the Alphas, Cole. And Nico, you get to meet with the coven. So good luck with that," I said, rolling my eyes.

"I'm so excited," Nico said deadpan.

"You should just come with me. You'll probably get more work done trying to wrangle Alphas that we don't know very well versus dealing with people who aren't going to speak to you at all."

"The Alphas from one of the Eastern Packs doesn't want mates involved because I'm pretty sure he's in a fight with his mate," Nico corrected. "So Adalyn and I aren't invited."

"Which I understand. We're Alpha's mates, not technically Alphas."

"We still call you Alpha. So people are just going to have to get the fuck over it," Cole added menacingly.

I went up to my tip toes and kissed him softly.

"Thank you for taking care of me. But I have to go, too. I promised Cassius I would work with him, and Dara needs a few things."

"She better not need any more of your blood," Cole said, though it was more of an order. I didn't blame him. When he had learned what exactly had begun the antidote process, he hadn't been happy that I had willingly given up a drop of blood to make it happen.

"For all we know, the vampires can somehow tie it back and hurt those who gave the blood. We don't know how their magic works. I don't like this."

"Of course you don't like it. But she doesn't need my blood anymore. That was just the catalyst to begin things. Now she can work from there. I'm okay."

"I don't like it," he continued to growl.

"You don't have to like it. But you do have to get over it."

"Burn," Nico said, as we each headed to the restroom to get ready for the day. I had washed my hair the night before, so I quickly took a shower so I didn't smell like sex and wolf that wasn't me for my meeting and training.

The guys each did the same, and we were careful to shower separately. We didn't do well showering together. Mostly because I spent too much time on my knees with someone's dick in my mouth, and the person behind me making me come. We were very good at that.

And it wasn't just the mating urge pushing us. It was my need for these two. Because they were mine. And I liked it.

I was just getting used to what that meant.

I put my hair in a messy ponytail, slid into torn-up jeans, boots, and a tank-layered jean top.

"You're looking specifically menacing today. I like it," Nico said, as he smacked my ass before he went to put on his leather jacket.

I narrowed my gaze at him, then licked my lips at the sight of him in that jacket.

"Stop drooling. We have places to be," Cole teased before he handed me my own jacket.

"But doesn't Nico look sexy as hell in that?" I asked.

"He does. But we can peel it off him later."

"You guys say the sweetest things. Who's going with you to the Aspens?" Nico asked.

I frowned and tried to remember. "I think Jacqueline. I have to look at the rotation. It's whoever also has things to do with the Aspen Pack den so that way we're not taking people off our own patrols."

Nico nodded. "Makes sense."

"And I don't want to run us ragged. We need to have a life of our own. We need our cubs and pups to feel as if they actually have a future."

I went up on my tip toes, cupped his slightly bearded face, and kissed him softly.

"I've always been a warrior, my Alpha. I will protect our people. I promise you that. We just need to find out exactly how Valac seems to know what we've been doing lately."

Cole frowned, and Nico gave a tight nod.

"He's been one or two steps ahead of us this whole time, even after losing his damn mind over his mate. I don't want to think that we have a mole."

"We can't look at our people as traitors. Not when they're connected to us through those bonds. You feel the bonds of Alpha's mates. In order to hide that level of treachery from us? They'd have to be dark of soul indeed."

"I know. I don't like the thought of that either. But I'm not quite sure what else there is to consider. It's not like he's using a technological bug or something to figure out what we're up to. To find our training paths, our patrol routes. I don't like the fact that he knew exactly how to get to the mountain in order to try to tear it down."

"I don't like any of that either, but the moment we go towards treachery, the moment we start to think our Pack isn't trustworthy, that is the moment that we truly start to let the vampires win."

"We're not the old Centrals," I whispered. "Just like we aren't the old Aspens. We are worthy to be here. We will find out who is doing this, if anyone. Or at least how

Valac is finding our moves. I promise you, Alpha mine. We'll figure it out."

Cole glared, but nodded tightly before he made his way out of the bedroom after giving us each a kiss good-bye. I looked at Nico helplessly, who just shook his head.

"You know more than anyone what he's going through. I don't want to think of our den and Pack betraying us, but Valac knows things. Things he shouldn't."

I nodded, knowing that this possibility was cruelly plausible. The fact that they always seemed to know our patrol lines, and where the Alphas meets were. It was worrying, but then again, just like Cole, I've lived through a legacy of betrayal.

"I don't have the same past that you and Cole do. I grew up with loving parents who went through hell and war, I've watched my family lose Blake, and I saw my family lose part of themselves when they did. So I've been on the other side. I don't want it to be true, but I also don't know what else there could be."

I hugged Nico tightly, knowing he still hurt thinking about his cousin who had died in battle when he fought alongside the Talons.

I hadn't been part of that, as Blade had forced us to stand back and not help out the Talons and Redwoods when they needed us. And I would never forgive myself for not being strong enough to do so anyway. But our four Packs were strength personified now. So we would find a way. I said my goodbyes, kissed Nico again, and sent a pulse of love down the bond hoping that Cole would feel it. I hadn't actually said the words to them, but I knew I was well on my way to falling. If I hadn't fallen already. I just needed a moment to breathe and think before I laid everything out there, laid myself bare.

Jacqueline and I were quiet in the car as we made our way there, two more soldiers in the back as they also wanted to train with Cassius and me. We had things on our mind, and the others were reading up on manuals. So we weren't ignoring each other.

We pulled into the Aspen den, that familiar yet home-sick magic making me smile. I liked the fact that I didn't feel unwanted, even though my new home was already a priority. It was a wonder, something I didn't think possible, but here I was, mated, pregnant, and in a different terri-tory that hadn't been my own.

"You're here," Dara said with a smile as I looked up at the witch. She looked exhausted, at least ten pounds lighter than she had at the beginning of the year. It worried me. She was putting too much of herself into the spells for the wards and the antidote. I glared at her, letting my wolf to the surface, and she held up her hands, a smile playing on her face.

"I swear every dominant wolf that walks past me growls at me, and every submissive wolf won't meet me in the eyes and hands me a cupcake. Or some food. I'm okay. I promise."

"Don't lie," I whispered.

She met my gaze and smiled, her eyes sad. "I'm not lying to you. I'll be okay. We've found an antidote. So we're going to find a way to strengthen the wards without my soul magic."

"We need more witches. For every den."

Dara nodded. "Hopefully Nico can pry some out of the coven today."

I winced and shook my head. "I don't think that's going to happen today. I think today is more of a meeting to get a meeting done."

Dara scowled. "Of course. Because that's always what happens. They're all councils about meetings and meetings about meetings. More worried about the power they control than what they can actually do with that power to protect."

"I wish there was something I could do. I'm so sorry."

Dara shook her head. "They're not going to listen to me, and they're sure as heck not going to listen to you. The new coven is very particular."

"I miss the old one."

Dara smiled softly. "The old one was a little better, but I was still not part of it."

I frowned.

"What? But our friends were part of the coven, at least on the outside."

"And that qualification is exactly it. Our friends were part of the council structure. Connecting to the coven. But they were Pack first. Just like I am. So no. I was never coven. I'm not an elemental witch. Despite what others may desire."

I frowned. "I'm so sorry."

"You did nothing but be my friend. I don't need anything else other than that. Now, we have to go meet with Lily and the others. I promised them I would let them know as soon as you were here."

"Sounds good, but I'm not allowed to give any blood."

Dara rolled her eyes. "I promise. Your blood is safe with me. Your Alphas don't need to growl at me anymore."

My eyes widened. "They growled at you?"

"Just once, and it was in passing. They didn't threaten me or anything. But I know the rules. Don't touch an Alpha's mate. Especially not an Alpha's pregnant mate."

I frowned, annoyed.

"I'm a dominant wolf, a soldier first. They don't get to tell me what to do."

Dara's eyes widened.

"Maybe not, but they're your mates and newly mated, and Cole is a freaking Alpha. If he wants to yell at me for hurting you by taking even a drop of blood, it's within his right."

I scowled. "Oh, I think the boys and I have very different ideas on that."

"Just don't put me in the middle of it. Don't think I can take that."

I reached out and squeezed Dara's hand. "I'm sorry. You don't have to take any of that."

"I know. Now, let's head over." She took a step forward and the wards buckled. I reached out and gripped her hand, keeping her steady. I looked up to see an oily sheen covering the wards of the den like a bubble. I didn't have a connection to the den anymore. I wasn't Aspen.

The alarm sounded and people started moving, and I turned, following the others. Dara scowled at me. "Your mates wouldn't want you running full force into this."

We didn't even know what *this* was. I glared at my friend. "You're the one who just was hurt by the wards being attacked, don't get me started."

Chase and Cruz were up front, sliding through the wards as a group of vampires being controlled by other vampires came forward. At least fifty of them. Bloody clothes, their eyes red, and I nearly tripped. Because to have that many newly made vampires at once meant that they were making even more than we thought.

I stared numbly, before I slid through the wards like the others and began to fight.

I ducked underneath the claws of one vampire, slid my own claws through its neck and decapitated it. These were young, weak, and it worried me. Because they weren't fighting as a unit. In fact, it only took the first round of soldiers ten minutes to take care of them all.

I knew this had to be a distraction. I turned and looked at Dara, still inside the wards, her eyes wide, blood pouring from her ears.

It wasn't the vampires that were the problem. No, it was the wards themselves.

Whatever had hit the wards first had been the initial attack. That was what they had wanted.

Because Dara was directly attached to the wards of the Aspen Pack. I ran towards her, sliding back through the wards that cut like glass into my skin. I caught her as she fell.

She shivered, her body seizing as Wren came forward, hands outstretched to heal.

There was nothing to heal as this was magical.

The vampires had thrown their magic at the wards and were hurting my friends, hurting my people.

And there was nothing we could do.

They were stronger than us. And no matter how hard we tried to be just as strong, there were things we didn't know, lines we wouldn't cross.

And my friends were the ones taking the brunt of the pain because of it.

SEVENTEEN

Cole

Bᴀᴛᴀ ᴛᴏBy the time Adalyn came home from the Aspens, my wolf was ready to shred anyone in front of us.

I had been on the line with Chase when the attack occurred, had watched his eyes narrow as he turned off the screen, presumably to run towards the attack on their wards. An attack that none of us exactly understood.

I had been left with no recourse when my mate had been out there, and I knew she would be on the front lines. I knew that no matter how much I wanted her to stay back and let others handle it, she wouldn't do that.

Because that was my damn mate.

"Don't growl at her as soon as she walks in the door," Nico whispered, and I whirled on him.

"She could have died. And we weren't there."

"You're never irrational, Cole. Why are you acting that way now?"

"Our mate and child could have died, and we were dealing with the rest of the world and not being with our mate. Why aren't you angry as hell right now? Why aren't you throwing things?"

"Because that's not going to help anything," Nico snapped. He stood right in front of me, his eyes glowing gold with his wolf. "Until Adalyn is in our arms, there's nothing I can do to calm my wolf down. So egging it on and raging over something I can't control just makes things worse."

"How did they hurt the Aspen wards?" I asked again, and Nico shook his head. "I don't know. The coven wouldn't even meet with me today. They claimed it was an emergency, but they're not even there."

I froze. "Do you think they're working with the vampires?" The thought had occurred to me before, but for some reason it hit harder now.

Nico shook his head. "I don't know. And that's what worries me."

"We'll talk with Adalyn when she gets here."

The bond tugged between the three of us. I met Nico's gaze and stormed out of the house, Nico right behind me.

I noticed that Nico didn't hold me back, and I had a feeling that his bravado was all for show.

Adalyn got out of the car while Lane ran towards Jacqueline, hugging her mate tightly. The other two Aspen soldiers who had been there to train and had fought alongside her, lowered their gazes and walked past me, nodding tightly.

They were uninjured, and while part of me wanted to reach out and hug them, to let them know that I was okay and grateful they were there, I needed to speak with my mate first, and that meant I needed to let the anger slide. I would go to them later, ensure they were safe.

But for now, it was all I could do not to throw Adalyn over my shoulder and tuck her inside and never let her out.

Her jaw tightened, but Nico brushed past me, and enveloped her in his arms.

"You're safe."

She hugged him tightly, patted his back, and pulled away.

"Of course I am. I was always safe."

"Don't fucking lie," I growled.

"Then don't growl at me. I was safe because the vampires weren't coming after me. They wanted the wards. And perhaps even to hurt Dara."

"Is Dara okay?" Nico asked.

"She will be. She's resting now. But she lost a lot of blood and was weakened by whatever Valac and the others hit the wards with."

223

"Did you see Valac?" I asked.

She shook her head. "No, I didn't. No one did. So maybe he isn't the one who sanctioned this. But it was the vampires. We fought them. I fought them."

I noticed the blood on her clothes and growled.

"Don't growl at me. I'm fine. I didn't even get hurt."

"But you could have. You're covered in fucking blood."

I knew I sounded unreasonable, like I was losing my damn mind. But my mate could have died today. What the hell was I supposed to do about that? Of course, I was going to want to hide her away from this. It wasn't fair that she had to be part of it at all.

"Let's take you inside, clean off the blood," I ordered. I knew it was the wrong thing to say, the wrong tone. But it was either that, or growl and scream and do something that I was going to regret.

Valac and the others continued to harm my mates. No matter what I did, it didn't seem to be enough. And I hated the fact I wasn't strong enough to stop it.

She stared at me, tilting her head in the way of the wolf.

No, we're not going to do this.

"You guys. Let's just go inside and talk."

She held up her hands to both of us.

"Nico, love, you might be doing your best to keep calm and sound as if you're not as growly as this one over here, but I can feel it along the bond. I can feel the absolute rage. But below that, I can feel the overprotectiveness that will suffocate me if you're not careful."

"We can't help who we are, Adalyn. You can't force us to change."

"I'm not weak. I'm a soldier. I always have been. I'm a dominant wolf, and that's not going to change. I'm unsure why you think that you can."

"You were almost killed!" I shouted. "More than once. And I'm just supposed to stand by and let that happen? I'm the damn Alpha and I can't even keep my mates safe. Nico was almost killed in the fucking landslide, and yet I'm supposed to act as if everything is normal?"

"Of course, nothing is normal. We're in a war, but we have been for nearly my entire life. We're dominant wolves. It is what we do. There are always forces out there who want to take what we have, to change who we are. If it's not this, then it's something else. But you can't change who I am. You can't change the power within my veins. I am not weak. Don't pretend that I am, and don't treat me like I'm fragile."

"We don't think you are fragile. You know we don't."

"Then don't lie to me. You guys are so angry that I would dare try to protect my friends, my former Pack, that you can't even look me in the eyes and hug me and tell me that you're glad that I'm here. Because that may be true, but you can't see past your anger and possessiveness to do anything about it. We are the Alpha triad. The first of its kind that I know of. And yet what are you doing? What do you believe in? I'm not sure. But it worries me. You worry me. So you two need to think about what you want. What you want this to be. Because there was no going back the moment the moon goddess decided we were mates and took that choice from us. And I've done my best to look forward into what we could have. I thought I was taking it in stride. But we need to figure out what this mating means. We don't get to back away. Because we are in charge of this den. Of this Pack. They are leaning on us, expecting us to protect them and actually know what we're doing. And beyond that? I'm *pregnant*. There is a baby growing inside me right now and we haven't even talked about it."

"Yes, we have," I growled, my wolf pacing. "We talked about it."

"In the idea sense. But what are we going to do? Are we going to stay in this house? Are we going to add onto it? Because there's not room for the three of us, let alone a new life. Have we talked about names? Have we celebrated anything? We haven't even had a mating ceremony. We've done nothing except move on, battle after battle, and I completely understand that. I completely understand what we've had to do in order to protect our people and try to figure out this new way of life. Yes everything is backwards, but I would like *something*. Just something. And maybe your faith in me needs to be first."

And with that she walked away. I stepped forward, she whirled away.

"I need space. Just give me one minute of damn space. I'm within the wards. I'm safe. Just let me breathe."

She slid through the forest and I staggered back, leaning against Nico's side.

"You fucked up," he whispered.

"I didn't even realize that we hadn't even planned a ceremony. We haven't met with your family, or Dawn," I said, speaking of my sister. "I know that Adalyn's family passed away, but we haven't had dinner with the Aspens or anything. We have just moved from step to step and training to training and we've done nothing."

I turned on him. "I love you, Nico. I've loved you as a friend for longer than I care to admit. But I love you. Beyond the mating bond. And I'm sorry that I haven't shown it."

"Cole."

"No. I've loved you before the mating bond happened. I love your passion, your strength. And I thought to myself that I'd have to find a way to venture on as an Alpha watching you and Adalyn become mates. Finding yourself. I didn't realize that it could be us three. And now we need to go find our mate and show her. Not just tell her."

"You're right. She deserves more than what we've given her."

"Time. I think she deserves time."

"I'll call my mom. And my sister. She can start with the Redwood side."

"Dawn can work with the Talons, and they'll call Audrey. She'll work with the Aspens."

"Goddess, I'm not good at this." I ran my hands over my face, and Nico moved forward and brushed my hair from my forehead.

"You don't have to always be good at things. You have us to rely on now. But you have to rely on us."

I swallowed hard, knew he was right, and let out a breath.

We needed to fix this.

I just didn't know how.

So we turned towards the woods, and I rolled my shoulders back.

"I think I need to grovel."

"And then we can start on everything else."

I tangled my fingers with Nico's and we ran towards our mate, knowing that if we didn't fix this, this would only be the tipping point.

CHAPTER
EIGHTEEN

Nico

I HAD TAKEN MY MATES FOR GRANTED, AND I NEEDED to fix that. Cole and I were still finding our way around, learning who we were together, and even though the attraction had always been there, we now needed to realize who we were as partners.

We followed Adalyn's scent, her trail evident. She wasn't trying to hide it from us. And she could. It was what she was good at. Hiding and lying in wait to attack those who threatened our den. Our people.

But she had left a trail for us. She wanted us to follow her. So we would.

"I love you too, you know," I whispered.

Cole, the graceful and powerful Alpha next to me, tripped over his feet and used a branch to catch himself.

"What?"

My lips twitched, even as my wolf paced, wanting Adalyn as well. She needed to be part of this. "I love you. I've always loved you. Which was kind of the problem. I've always wanted you, loved you, and I think the moon goddess was tired of us pussyfooting around."

Cole tugged on my hand and I turned towards him.

"We need to do better about this. We're so worried about the bigger picture, I think we missed everything else."

I smiled and leaned forward to kiss him softly. We were nearly the same height, so it was easy to do, and I was grateful for that.

His lips were soft, his beard rough against my skin. He was so damn dominant, it sent shivers down my body. Oh, I might be dominant as well, but there was just something about Cole that changed everything for me.

I pulled away, both of our eyes glowing gold, and we turned to make our way towards Adalyn.

She stood in wolf form at the edge of a small creek. She leaned down, drinking, before she looked over at us, her eyes narrowing. She was a gorgeous gray wolf, with white paws and gold eyes.

I had always loved her in wolf form. Her grace. The way that she looked, nothing like I would have imagined. Because with her wild hair, auburn in the sunlight, I would have thought she would be a red wolf. But no, she was majestically gray with silver streaks, and looked stunning.

She tilted her head and fluffed her tail at us, as if beckoning us to follow her. So I began to strip without even thinking.

Cole let out a chuff, before stripping off his shirt next to me.

The change was swift and beautiful and painful all at once. As the magics changed within the world, so did our shifts. It was no longer fifteen or twenty minutes of agonizing pain. Instead it was shorter with each passing year. Part of me knew we probably should be worried about what that meant. What else could change within the magics of our Packs? But right then, if it led me to being closer with Adalyn and Cole in a timely fashion I would allow it. And I wouldn't think about the worry. At least, not yet.

Cole finished shifting faster than me but only by a few moments. My magics were evening out, my connection to my wolf different than it had been before. I didn't know if it was because of who I was with my two mates, or if it was because I was connecting with my powers more.

I pranced towards Adalyn and she let out a huff of a laugh. She grinned at me in a way only another wolf could, and I held back a smile of my own. I rubbed my body against hers as Cole did the same to her other side, and she shivered between us.

That bond that connected us changed ever so slightly. Maturing. Or maybe that was just hope.

She charged off then, into the woods, and we followed, our mate at the forefront, and though during this run I would always be on the watch, careful for danger, I would not force my mate into a position where she felt as if she was nothing. I would never do that again. I would never make her feel that she was anything less than power personified.

At least, I would try. I wasn't always the best at doing what I needed to, after all.

We moved through the forest, this path different than one I was used to. Because I was in a new den, a new Pack. I didn't know every inch of this land yet, but I would. And I would protect it with everything that I was.

We jumped over another broken log, and my heart ached because I knew that newly shorn tree was because of the landslide. So much destruction to the earth and to the souls of our people because of the power-hungry madness of a vampire, and perhaps something more.

But I couldn't think about all of that right then, not when I needed to focus on the smaller picture. Just like I had said before. No longer focusing on everything that wasn't the three of us in this moment.

We ran until our wolves tired and our breaths came in pants. I was in love with my mates. Both of them. And I needed to show it, rather than being afraid to be the vulnerable witch and wolf that I was.

When we finally made our way back to where we had stashed our clothes, Cole rubbed his body against mine and then playfully nipped at Adalyn. I did the same, and she rolled those gold eyes of hers before she moved to the side, and the magic of the shift began to take over. I did the same, biting back the pain from shifting so quickly. I wouldn't be able to shift again for a while, not unless I replenished my energy. Cole would probably be able to, as he was more dominant than both of us, but I wouldn't want him to. I wouldn't want him to weaken himself when we could also fight in human form.

When we were all changed, sweat-slick, and out of breath, Adalyn turned to us.

"I'm sorry for running away. I shouldn't have done that."

I shook my head. "No, it's okay. We weren't treating you the way that we should have. And that's on us."

I cupped her face, her naked breasts pressing against my chest. I growled, wanting more, but I knew I needed a moment to think.

"I'm sorry. So sorry that we made you feel that you weren't strong. I never want to be that person for you. I never want you to think that you can't do anything."

"I know that," she said with a roll of her eyes. "I want to blame the hormones, but I think it's my own insecurities."

She pulled away and faced us. "I didn't even think about a mating ceremony. Who am I? I love you both. But

I've been so afraid to say that because I realized that I've loved you long before the moon goddess decided we needed to be together. And maybe if we would have actually faced who we were before that, it wouldn't have come as such a shock. I'm so worried that we lost all this time because of fear, of who we were, of the mistakes that we made in the past. I don't want to make those same mistakes with you guys. With anyone. So don't let me, okay? Just be with me. We'll figure out our future with this child. With this new life. With us. Everything's coming at once and maybe we're not doing it in the right order or how we should, but I'm tired of feeling behind. I just want to move forward. With both of you."

I crushed my lips to hers, knowing there wasn't much left to say. Cole came to her other side and hugged us both, as we stood there naked, the three of us taking turns with one another so each of us could kiss, could feel.

"I'm sorry. So sorry," Cole whispered.

"Don't be sorry. I'm the one who can't keep up with my own emotions."

I growled. "It's the blood in your veins, as in ours, the strength in our souls. We can face whatever we need to. But first, we should probably face each other."

She looked down between us, my hard cock pressing against her stomach. "I think we're pretty much facing."

I laughed as she rolled her eyes. "That's not exactly what I meant."

"I want a mating ceremony. I want the world to see that we chose each other. Okay?"

"Of course. I choose you. I will always choose the both of you."

Cole cleared his throat. "Now you're taking my lines, Jamenson."

I winked at my mate. "You're just going to have to be faster."

"Speaking of fast," Adalyn whispered, as she stood between us, sliding her hands down both of our cocks. I groaned, thrusting into her hold.

"I was thinking we could go soft and slow, to cherish this moment with each other."

She squeezed my dick, and my eyes crossed.

"How about fast and hard in proving how much we want each other? You can play Princess and the Pea later. I just want you both. My wolf wants you both. I want to choose you both. Now go ahead, fuck me. I need you."

With those words, Cole slid his hands between her legs and rubbed her clit.

I grinned, wrapped my hand around her neck, and forced her face to mine. I crushed my mouth to hers, both of us groaning at the sensation. She was still rubbing my cock, and as I stepped forward, she rubbed my dick against Cole's, and I shivered. The sensation was almost too much, but I wasn't about to come in her hand so quickly. No, I needed something more than that.

We continued to explore, to kiss, to taste. When I

moved forward to wrap my hand around Cole's, we plunged our fingers deep inside her. She let out a shocked breath, shaking as she came.

"You both are so big at the same time," she whispered.

I grinned. "Oh, I'm glad you said that because right now is only the beginning."

Her eyes widened. "Um, I think we're missing a key component for that."

"I might have some in my pocket," I whispered.

I gestured towards the pile of clothes and she blushed. "You just carry that around with you?"

"We are newly mated in a triad. Yes, I carry that around with me." I kissed her again, and we were both lost.

We lay on the bed of leaves made for us by Mother Nature herself as I delved between her legs with my mouth. We groaned as she swallowed Cole whole, cupping his balls and playing with him. And to finish out the triad that we made, Cole lay on his side, sucking me off, swallowing me deeply.

I could barely keep my breath straight, keep anything straight in that moment.

All that mattered were my mates touching me, and when we pressed into each other, flaring alone the bond, we came, shaking.

I rocked my hips into Cole's mouth, him swallowing every drop of me, as Addy's thighs tightened around my face, her orgasm beautiful as it flushed her entire body.

I kept moving, wanting more, and when Cole reached

for the lube, instead of working on either one of us, he slid his hand between Adalyn's thighs and worked on her opening.

Her eyes widened and she grinned, and I knew it was time for that step. Something that we had talked about, something that we needed.

Cole readied her as I continued to play with her pussy, her nipples, her mouth. As we were shifters, Cole and I were already hard again, waiting, wanting. I lay on my back as Adalyn moved to straddle me. My warrior princess, my guardian.

"Are you ready?"

She nodded, her eyes gold.

"I want both of you. I'm ready. I've been craving this."

I pressed my thumb along her clit, as she slowly, oh so slowly, sank down onto my cock.

I shivered. My body going taut as she sank down on me completely. When she began to move, I gripped her hips, keeping her steady.

"Almost, darling. Almost. Let's make sure you're ready for Cole."

"You're so big, it's going to be hard to fit you both."

"I think we can make it, Addy."

She grinned and kissed me softly as she leaned over me, my dick still wrapped within her. I spread her for Cole, as he continued to lube himself and her, and we both groaned at the sensation of his fingers deep inside her as my cock was buried in her pussy. Cole slowly pressed his cock at her ass, and Adalyn froze.

"Are you ready?" I whispered. "We can stop."

She shook her head. "I'm ready. Please. Fill me. Take me. I'm yours."

I smiled, then winked over her shoulder at Cole, who gently began to press deep inside her.

"Oh, my God. I can't breathe. You're both too much."

We froze, and then she shook her head. "No, keep going. I want this. Just, wow. You both are a lot."

"Anytime you want to stop, we can. This is for you and us, but for you."

"I trust you both." She looked down at me, her eyes wide, full of everything that I wanted and craved. "I love you both."

I captured her lips, and then as Cole slid deeper inside her, he leaned down and he kissed me as well. He pressed kisses along Adalyn's back, and when we were finally ready, Cole and I moved. We took turns, taking her slowly. This wasn't the hard and fast that we had joked about. No, this was a gentle caress that turned into heat and stretching, tension and more. This was everything, and nothing, and yet the world at once.

A moment in time that could change passion forever with just one breath.

This was our moment, our forever. My moment, my mates'.

And when Adalyn came, her body writhing on us, her

words incoherent, she clamped down around my cock and I filled her, my body shaking with my orgasm. Cole followed suit, and the three of us held onto one another for dear life as the goddess blessed us again, our mating bond strengthening beyond anything that I had ever felt before.

This was what I had been missing. A promise. A single moment in time that was just for us.

Because the world could come after us, and it would.

But right then, the only thing that mattered was each other. Our Pack. Our world.

This was what we had been missing. Not just sex. Not just this connection. But peace. Time where we weren't fighting, when we weren't planning.

Where we just had each other.

And I would fight to the end of the world to have this happen again. To keep this moment. To keep them safe.

I just didn't realize that chaos would come so quickly.

That the world could end in a moment.

And that we wouldn't be ready.

CHAPTER
NINETEEN

Cole

"I can't believe it took us this long to gather and have dinner, but then again, we've been a little busy." Hannah, Nico's mother, winked before she hugged me close. I swallowed hard and hugged her back, feeling slightly out of my depth.

Dawn, my sister, came up to me and hugged us both.

"Look at us, a big family. Although technically I feel like I'm already connected to you guys through other family members."

"It's going to get a little confusing when our kids are like eighth cousins at this point."

I snorted at my brother-in-law's pronouncements and rolled my eyes.

"Well, we're running out of Jamensons and Redwoods to mate with, and all of your siblings are mated. So we should be okay," I corrected.

"That's good to know," Hannah said. "Oh, I still have a couple more children left who are searching for their mates. And you're making me a grandmother. I still can't believe that." She beamed as she said it, looking like a gorgeous woman in her late twenties. Hannah stopped aging when she mated Reed and Josh over thirty years ago. Her life was tied to the life of the wolf in the mating triad. It wasn't the same for shifters who mated, as we were already long-lived. I knew that some witches later would go through the painful and deadly process of becoming a shifter so that way their lives would be long-lived on their own, but not everybody wanted that. Especially with their children full grown now, I didn't think Hannah, Josh, and Reed wanted to contemplate living in a world without each other.

Considering I was just now realizing what that meant to me and my mates, who happened to be shifters in their own right, I understood their decision.

But I didn't really want to think about the possibility.

She went off to speak with more of their children, since Nico had six siblings and was the middle child. I stood by Dawn and put my arm around her shoulders.

"Hello, Talon Pack member."

She rolled her eyes at me. "Oh shush."

"What? You're the mate of the Beta of the Talon Pack. You're all-powerful."

"You say that, and you're Alpha. With two mates. You just had to outdo me, didn't you, brother?"

I shrugged. "Your brother-in-law is the Supreme Alpha of us all. I don't think that our family connections can be outdone."

"You are right in that," she said with a laugh. "I'm so proud of you. Happy for you. All of that. You are amazing. And I'm blessed that I am your sister. And you're making me an aunt."

That made me grin. "Where's baby Callum? I thought that he would be here."

She shook her head. "We decided to leave him with his aunties and uncles. Not that the Central Pack isn't safe, I can promise you that."

She must have seen the worry in my gaze and went to kiss my cheek.

"Seriously, you're amazing and I love you. It's more that we wanted this to be an adults-only time. Our little date night to hang out with my family."

"I'm glad that you're here. So we have Redwoods with Nico's family, although I'm kind of glad that we didn't invite his entire family. All those aunts and uncles and cousins and second cousins wouldn't be able to fit in my house."

She laughed. "True. So, are you going to build something new? For the new baby?"

I nodded. "We're going to build near here. This will be a good place for a young soldier to move into. I didn't take the biggest building, where we could all meet up. But now I want to do that, to have a center and a home for us."

"You're a good man. And an even better Alpha."

"I don't feel that all the time. But thank you, sister mine."

"It's my pleasure. Now, I see that Adalyn brought Chase and Skye with her. So Nico's cousin is still part of this, and I'm glad that Adalyn had family to bring."

"I know that some of the other Aspen members wanted to come, and will when we have a baby shower or something. Oh God, do I need a baby shower?" I asked, nearly tripping over my words.

Dawn threw her head back and laughed as Adalyn came strolling through, ginger ale in her hand. She had been nauseous all day and scowled when everybody wanted to help. She was just going to have to get over that. We were going to help no matter what.

"Are you doing okay, mate?" I asked, holding out my hand. She took it, squeezed it, and then leaned into me. "I'm fine. I'm no longer nauseous, but I was craving this. Am I going to need ginger ale for this entire pregnancy? That wouldn't be too bad."

"I craved peanut butter. Apparently, I was cliché all the way."

"You also craved strawberry cupcakes. With lemon cream cheese frosting. Only that combination, though," Mitchell corrected from the other side of the room.

Dawn scowled, turning a little green. "Oh God, don't mention those. I ate so many."

"That actually sounds kind of good," Adalyn said with a smile. "Although I cannot bake."

"I can't either," I added, thinking about how I was going to keep up with Adalyn's cravings. I would do anything for her, but I probably should learn how to cook.

"I've got you covered," Nico said as he came up between us, wrapping his arm around Dawn's shoulder to give her a kiss on the top of her head. We were all friends, warriors that had fought together for years. It was nice just to be here, a moment of peace during a time of torment and chaos.

"You can cook? You've only made a few things at the house, but nothing really from scratch."

Nico shrugged. "Mom and Dads made sure I knew how to cook. They wanted to ensure we all knew."

I looked down at Adalyn, who blushed. "Yeah, I didn't get that memo."

"Me either."

"I taught myself, but it took a few burned dinners in order to get it right," Dawn said.

"And we've mostly been eating small meals or with the rest of the Pack in the commissary and dining hall. Our cooks and chefs there are great at what they do, and I haven't had time for me to make you a nice dinner. But I will. And I can bake, too."

Adalyn threw her arms around him and he staggered back while I just laughed at the two.

"Of course, now I feel like we're going to have to test his skills," I said into the laughter, and Dawn looked up at me.

"You're happy. I love that you're happy."

"I love that you all are here."

I knew we wouldn't always be able to do this, to take time out for ourselves when there was so much to do, but this was what was needed for a healthy Pack and den. We had a Pack dinner coming up soon, where those not on patrol would be able to enjoy time together, and eventually we would have our mating ceremony. There were a few other mating ceremonies to have first though, and that brought my wolf and me so much joy that everything just seemed to make sense.

My phone buzzed, and I looked down at it, frowning.

"Crap," I mumbled.

"What is it?" Dawn asked as everyone stared at me.

"It's Lane and Jacqueline. Their car won't start, and she has a wolf that just finished treatment in the city in the back. She needs my power, and I need to get closer to do that as they get the car fixed."

"You're not going alone," Nico growled.

"I won't. I promise. I'll take one of my sentries. I

wanted to go with Robert anyway. He needs to go for a run as it is."

"Are you sure that's safe?" Chase asked, and I nodded.

"They're only a mile outside the wards. And we can't be stuck within them forever. I'll be fine, I promise." I kissed both of my mates and said my goodbyes, knowing I would be back soon.

Robert was outside on patrol when I met him, and he agreed to come with me, and we both headed out on foot towards Lane and Jacqueline.

There were others that could have gone to this, but Lane must have been exhausted from the surgery. She was using too much of herself, as Healers did. And if Jacqueline couldn't fix the car herself, she was probably growly as all get out.

We turned the corner and made it to the car, as Jacqueline stood at the hood, snarling at it.

"I'm sorry for ruining your dinner, but Lane needs you, and I can't carry them both."

"It's okay. I promise." I nodded as Robert went to help Jacqueline with the car and I opened the back of the SUV to see Jacqueline kneeling behind a stretcher.

I cursed under my breath. "Why didn't you tell me it was this bad?" I whispered.

"It's that old vampire bite. He's better, but had a bad reaction to one of the meds when he was under. And he was already going in to have his gallbladder out later, so it just escalated. He's fine. I just need a few bits of your energy if that's okay."

Concerned, I put my hand on her shoulder, letting her have some of my Alpha's energy and power. Not all Alphas could do this, but I could. The stronger I was, the stronger they could be. She could have everything she wanted of mine in order to survive because that was all that mattered.

The young man lying down in the back gasped in a breath before his eyes opened.

"Alpha," he whispered before he fell asleep.

Lane sank down into me, and I hugged my Healer close.

"Use too much?" I asked.

"Yes, but it's fine. I'll do better next time."

"You're damn straight you will."

"Thanks for bringing Robert. I needed an extra two hands that knew what they were doing to fix that engine. It annoys the hell out of me, I couldn't do it myself."

I shook my head, then jumped out of the car.

"Come on, let's head back. My mates are waiting for me."

Jacqueline grinned. "And my mate needs to go to bed."

"My patient's doing well, so yes, bed sounds great."

The two women looked at each other as Robert laughed before everything went dark.

Somebody screamed, an explosion rang out, and blood splattered on Robert's face before there was nothing.

"HE'S WAKING UP. FINALLY."

I slid open my eyes at the voice, wondering what the hell had just happened.

I looked around the dark room, wondering how the hell I had gotten here before everything started to come back to me.

Robert, falling to his knees, half of his face gone. The intense lack of scent around us, as if everything had been taken away. That's why we hadn't noticed someone had snuck up on us.

Jacqueline's and Lane's screams as they moved. And someone smashing me upside the head with something long and metallic.

I focused on the dark room before lights blinked on, and I realized I was chained to a wall, my feet barely touching the ground, my shirt off and my jeans bloody.

They had taken my shoes, and I realized electrodes were touching the bottoms of my feet, my sides, my shoulders.

I knew exactly who had done this.

Valac walked into the room, his eyes red, his body sweat-slick. He didn't look good, yet he still looked damn strong. Too strong.

"Good. Good. You're awake. You're probably

wondering how I got you here. I have a few stories for you, dear Alpha."

I pulled against the chains trying to get to the man, but he just smiled at me.

"Stop. The more you move against the chains, the more you'll bleed. But there's no getting out of this. You screwed up. You didn't use your senses." Valac blinked, then snapped his fingers. "Oh wait. My new trusting little magical spell took away your senses. Just for an instant. And we were downwind far enough away we knew you wouldn't be able to scent us. That is how we took the Alpha of the Centrals. The weakest Alpha amongst them. You were our guinea pig. And now that we know we can take you, we know that we can take the others."

"Are you done listening to yourself talk? You're exhausting."

Valac reached out and slapped me, his claws out. Blood trickled down my face, and he narrowed his gaze at me.

"You sure do like talking a lot for a dead man."

"Funny, I was thinking the same about you."

Fear slid through me, but not for myself. Never for myself.

"Where are my people?" My voice was a low growl. I needed to sound in control, and nothing in me was in control. I shoved against the chains, but they were magical in nature, that much I knew. They dug into my skin, and I had no idea what those electrodes would do.

I didn't think they were there to monitor me.

"Your little wolf, the guard dog? He got in our way. He was just slightly upwind, and well, you saw his blood. There's no coming back from that. The others are safe though. We didn't need the two women and their weak little wolf. They can go back to your den and tell them that we took their Alpha. They need to know the truth. That once you take something from me, you lose everything."

I growled.

"It seems to me that you don't have much. Not if you have to resort to dark magic and losing your soul in order to take me down."

Valac threw his head back and laughed. "You try so hard, and yet all you do is make mistake after mistake, and realize that you can't take me. You didn't even realize that I was behind you. You didn't even realize I had killed your man until blood sprayed across his face. The world will know what happens when you touch what's mine!" Valac screamed and pressed the button next to the doorway. Electricity shocked my system, slamming into me. I arced off the wall, trying to break through my chains as pain sliced into me and I wanted to vomit.

And then Valac stopped and grinned, before he turned on the lights completely, illuminating what was on the other side of the glass I hadn't realized was to my right.

What I saw nearly sent me over the edge and I swallowed hard, my wolf shaking with rage. I wanted to shift, I needed to get out of there. But I couldn't. There was nothing I could do in that moment.

Two women that I knew and had fought alongside, sat strapped to chairs, tape over their mouths, their legs bound together. Lily, the little witch of the Aspen Pack, and Wynter, a human member, sat side by side, bruised, their eyes wide.

I thrashed against my bindings but Valac glared at me.

"I'll cut them. One cut at a time, and then I'll sink my fangs into their flesh. I won't turn them, but I will feast on them. I'll strip them of their skin, eat their flesh, and suck every ounce of blood that they have until they are rotting corpses, while you sit there and watch and know that you have failed. I will find every weak member of these Packs, and I will kill them. And I will force the Alphas to watch as I do."

"What is it you want? Because there has to be something you want, other than to see us bleed."

Valac pushed his hair from his face, his body far more gaunt than I had seen it.

"I want you to feel the pain I did when you took my Sunny. But that's just the first step. You didn't even know we existed for the years we roamed this planet. You didn't know that we were the ones in the dark, the nightmares that people screamed about. You thought you were the apex predators and you weren't. The humans are beginning to love you. To let you be part of their governments and lands. You have treaties with the damn mayor, deciding who can help with what issues that arise. You're in hospitals, you have plans for a better future. And yet none of you want payback for the decimation that occurred when the humans first found out about you. Some of your Packs are still in hiding, and yet you do nothing to bring them to heel. We will be the ones that rule the humans. We will be the ones that bring forth the new dimension and power. But first you have to learn to kneel."

I raised my chin. "I will never kneel for a monster."

Wynter screamed as a vampire slid out of the darkness and scraped his fangs along her arm. He didn't bite down, but I glared.

"How will my kneeling protect them? What would you have me do?"

Because I knew if I knelt, figuratively since I was literally chained to a wall, nothing would change. It wouldn't protect me. It wouldn't save them. We were dead no matter what, but if there was some way I could find out his plans and get it to the others, that would be enough.

They wanted all power, all governing bodies. It didn't seem feasible, but for all I knew perhaps they had far more reach than I could ever dream of. After all, they had already done so much to us.

"I just want you to bleed."

Wynter and Lily screamed through their tape again as electricity shot through my body, and then Valac smiled and I knew this was only the beginning.

They slammed more energy into me, and then the knives came out, slicing my skin inch by inch.

My wolf slammed into me, sending me strength. I needed to get out of this, but there was no way that I could.

Not like this.

All that mattered was getting to my mates, making sure Lily and Wynter were safe.

But I wasn't sure I could do it. Wasn't sure I could protect them.

They continued to cut into my body, and when Valac smiled, his hand full of black dust, I knew what was coming next.

And I knew I didn't have the antidote on me.

That black magic shard slid into my body, ice pricks into warm flesh. The magic bled into me, one breath, then the next, as a fiery explosion shocked my body and I screamed.

I would die from this. No matter how strong I was, no matter that I was the fucking Alpha, the witches' powers blended with the vampire magic and whatever else their leader held, meant that I would not survive alone. And the women in that other room would die, too.

So I screamed, weakened, and tried to fight back. I kicked and I shoved, and as a vampire hit the ground, another one stabbed me, and then another and another. I would not back down, but I wasn't enough.

And then there was quiet, oh so quiet, and they were letting me breathe.

And I slept.

Soft hands touched my face, and I awoke to Adalyn kneeling in front of me, her eyes wide. "Wake up. Wake up. We have the antidote."

"Mate," I whispered, my eyelashes fluttering, trying to open my eyes completely.

"You're fine. You're fine. I love you. Come on, wake up for us. Nico!"

"I'm on it."

Blood rushed into my arms as I was lowered to the ground and I winced, pinpricks of sensation shooting over me.

"We've got you. We've got you."

"The girls?"

Adalyn looked over my head and nodded tightly. "Wren is with them. So is Chase. The Aspens will take care of their girls, and I will take care of you. Come on. We've got you."

"The others in the car?" I asked.

Nico growled under his breath. "Lane and Jacqueline are home. Robert..." He bit off a curse as pain slammed into my heart. "Let us use the antidote. We need to protect you."

"Where's Valac?" I asked, energy slowly coming back even though my whole body ached.

"Valac left a trail a mile wide. We knew you were hurt along the bonds, and we did our best to find you. I think he wanted us to find you. He didn't kill you, nor the girls. He just wanted to prove that he could. Because he's a sadistic bastard."

I looked at Nico and swallowed hard. "He'll pay for hurting them."

"He's going to pay for a lot of things. Now go to sleep, my Alpha. We'll take care of you." Adalyn leaned down and kissed the top of my head and I leaned into my mates.

I was Alpha, I couldn't be weak, but in their arms I knew I could sleep. And heal.

And plan how to keep my people safe.

CHAPTER

TWENTY

Nico

"COLE IS SLEEPING?" I ASKED, FROWNING AS ADDY came towards me.

She nodded and gripped my hand. "Finally. I can't believe we got kicked out because of that grumpy wolf."

My lips twitched and I tried not to smile.

"Of course, we got kicked out. We are the worst when he's grumpy. Because we only agitate him. His wolf wants to take care of us because he's angry, and we want to take care of him because we're all dominant."

"So his sister and your mother being there will protect him. He'll get some sleep, and they can bully him into actually taking time for himself."

"They're good at that. We're going to have to learn."

"Maybe our future offspring will be good at that."

Addy pressed her hand over her belly and shook her head. "A few months from now, we're going to be parents. I cannot believe this. I'm still trying to come to terms with what happened last night."

I cupped her face and kissed her softly. "Let's go for a run. We have patrol tomorrow night, and I have a meeting with the coven later." Her lip curled into a snarl, and I barely held mine back.

"Are they actually going to meet with you, or are they just going to kick you out again?"

"They better meet with me. Because somebody is using magic with the vampires. And I hope to hell it's not the coven and it's just rogue witches."

"I wouldn't be surprised at either, actually. This new coven kicks out anybody they don't agree with. Anybody they don't like. So, of course, there's going to be powerful witches out there who don't agree with everything that the coven is doing."

"But that doesn't mean they have to go to the vampire side. Look at Dara. She came to our side."

"Not everybody has a Pack of wolves and other shifters to take care of them. It should be the coven doing it, and yet it's not. It's not the coven. So what does that mean?"

"It means that we're in trouble. A lot of damn trouble."

"I'll never get the image of Cole hurt out of my mind."

"I'm just adding it to the image of you strung up by your arms, thanks to Valac."

"Then I'll add it to the one of you standing in front of a wall of rocks and a landslide about to kill you. I think we're done fighting individually against these things. They're using dark magic. They have a fucking demon. We need to stop Valac once and for all."

I agreed with her, but there was nothing we could do in that moment. All we were doing was agitating our wolves. "Come on. Let's go for a run."

She smiled at me, and I remembered that I'd loved this woman for far longer than I'd let myself imagine. "I think that'd be good for the baby."

"It'd be good for me too," I grumbled before I patted her stomach and ducked out of the way of her fist. I laughed, and the two of us ran, stopping to talk to a few Pack members as we did. They all wanted to know about their Alpha and our plans for the future. Everyone knew about the baby now, knew about what was coming. And there was joy in their eyes.

While the Redwood Pack was settled and growing in its own magic, the Aspen Pack and the Centrals were relearning who they were. I knew Adalyn was used to this, but I wasn't. I liked being on the side of growth and learning. We kept moving, Adalyn slower behind me than usual. I turned, and she shook her head.

"I don't have morning sickness or nausea, but I don't know. I think I'm just tired."

I stopped abruptly in the middle of a grouping of trees and studied her face. "Do you want to go back? I'll carry you."

"I'm going to pretend you didn't just say that," she said with a laugh. She went to her tiptoes and kissed me softly. "Come on. Let's finish our run and let our wolves out. It's been a while with just the two of us. Cole is hurt and I'm all agitated. I need you."

My cock hardened and I held in a growl. "I'll never get over the fact that you just say what you want. There's no coyness in it. I love it."

"I couldn't say what I wanted for a long time. I had to hide who I was and my own strength. I had to pretend I was nearly submissive in order to protect my Pack. And while I love the submissives in my Pack, I'm not one. Their wolves strengthen and yearn to care for others, to be cared for. My wolf needed to protect, and I couldn't do that. So I will always do my best to say what I want and what I mean. I don't have it in me to do anything else anymore."

I gripped her hand and led her to the edge of the lake, the sunlight glistening off the water's edge. I like that we have time for the two of us, just like you have time with Cole, and so do I. I think we need the three of us."

"Honestly, we're all just hot messes. You keep us calm and rational, even though you don't think you're the one who is."

"I have all this magic running through me. I don't feel calm."

"But you're the voice of reason. Cole is the responsible one who overdoes it sometimes. And I'm the hothead. We make it work." She grinned, and I couldn't help but kiss her.

She smiled up at me as I moved back, and then I slowly backed her towards a tree. Her eyebrow winged up, but I just kissed her before I slid my hand up her soft dress and cupped her breast. She moaned, my thumb sliding over her bra, her nipple pebbling.

"Nico. I need you."

"I've always needed you," I whispered.

I'd always wanted her, and now she was mine. To share and to be mine. There was nothing more I needed.

"I'm so glad that you're wearing this."

"Oh?" She clutched the tree hard as I hiked her dress up and slid my hands beneath her panties. She moaned, her pussy wet and swollen. I played with her clit before inserting two fingers deep inside her, loving the way she clamped around me. She rocked into my hand, fucking herself. When she came, she shuddered out a moan. I kissed her shoulder, grateful that we had this moment together. Because I knew something bad was coming, just like I knew the magic within me would have to be ready. But I didn't think about that right then. I undid my jeans, lowered them just enough to free my cock, and pressed myself against her entrance.

"Do it already. Please. I need you. My wolf needs you."

My fangs elongated, wanting to mark her, so I tugged her dress down, baring one breast, my fangs at her throat. She grinned as I slammed into her. We froze before I started to move, fucking her as she arched into me, both of us out of breath, sweat-slick and needy.

This wasn't sweet. This wasn't two mates slowly learning one another. This was taking off the edge. Because our mate had been hurt and there was nothing we could do. Later we would cuddle with our mate, lick his wounds, and just ensure that he was safe.

And we would show the Pack we were safe. But until then, we needed to get this aggression out before we hurt ourselves and others. And fucking my mate hard against a tree was the best way I could think to do it.

"Harder. Please."

I obliged my mate, my warrior princess, and when we both came, the bond between us flared. I knew Cole was pushing back that heat and that love along the connection between the three of us.

Our mate missed us, and it made my lips quirk.

I pulled out of her and we panted together. I held her close, both of us still leaning against the tree for balance.

"Well then. That's one way to spend the afternoon."

I pushed her hair back from her face, studying her strong cheekbones and her catlike eyes.

"Do you feel better now?"

"Are you asking me if your magical cock saved me?" she asked dryly.

I barked out a laugh. "No, it's more that I knew your wolf was riding you, just like mine was. And we don't have time for a full run in our wolf forms. Not when you need to meet with the maternals, and I have to meet with the witches."

She rolled her eyes, kissed my jaw. "Fine. But you are our anchor. Just make sure you know that. My little foundation."

I bit her chin, and she yipped before we adjusted our clothing and walked hand in hand back to the den.

It was just a moment of peace, and it had to be. But that's all that I needed.

I stood outside the coven building, wondering when it had all gone wrong. The coven, the shifters, the humans, all of us, were supposed to work together to take down the vampires. To protect our world from outside threats and internal ones.

The coven was far older than I was, but the way that we worked as a council was newer. My age nearly.

"I'm sorry. But we can't help you," Anastasia said. "I wasn't even allowed to meet with the leader. I was just a witch-born wolf. Not good enough. Never good enough for them."

"You're kidding me. The coven has always worked with the council. We need you."

"You promised to help," Cruz growled beside me.

Cruz was the Aspen Pack representative today, while our Redwood Pack and Talon Pack reps stood on my other side. We all glared at Anastasia, who held up her hands, a witch-bound ward blocking us from entering the coven grounds even though we had been invited.

"We will not meet with the shifters. We will not help you. We have our own strife. This is your mess. You clean it up."

I had known this was coming, and yet it was still a blow. My wolf pushed at me, my magic bubbling, but I had to be in control.

Even if she wasn't.

"You're making a mistake."

Anastasia's eyes glowed with white light before she held out her palms, magic burning between them. It sang to my own magic and I nearly stepped forward, wanting to fight, but Cruz held me back. The fact that the hothead next to me was the one who held me back told me that this witch had done something.

"If you come back, we will consider it a declaration of war. And we witches do not want your war. But we have died countless times for you shifters. Our blood has been spilled to protect your precious homes, and you have done nothing for us. So fix this yourselves. We are done." And with that, she disappeared.

Literally disappeared behind her wards, and a growl slipped my lips.

"What the hell was that about?" Cruz asked.

I shook my head and looked at the three men. "It means the witches just picked a side, and it wasn't the right one. And we're fucked."

I didn't have any better words for that.

The power within my veins pulsed, and I knew we would have to find other witches soon. It wouldn't be today, it wouldn't be tomorrow, but the coven was a problem. But they weren't our priority. First would be Valac.

And then the magic.

And I was afraid to all hell that it wouldn't be enough. That both would combine, and our Packs would be lost.

TWENTY-ONE

Cole

"Okay, come on, old man. I know your knee is aching you, but that just means rain is coming."

I scowled at my friend and fellow Alpha, and Chase just laughed.

"I'm sorry. I know you're all healed."

I also know the other man was teasing because if we didn't laugh about it, our wolves would take over and we'd be a dominance nightmare. As it was, it was like walking on eggshells around my den right now. People wanted to comfort me, yet all my wolf wanted to do was growl at the vampires and comfort everyone in my wake.

"You're here to train, but how about we just talk?" Chase asked, and I chuffed out a breath.

"You know I haven't spoken a word recently. You're doing all the talking for the both of us."

My friend quirked a brow. "Because you're doing the silent and broody thing. Your mates are over in the other circle training right now, and every once in a while, you stop what you're doing and get all growly protective over both of them. If Adalyn ends up with a bruise after sparring with Cassius later, you will try to harm my Packmate, and then Adalyn and I will both have to beat your ass."

I laughed. "If Cassius's mate doesn't do it first."

"Novah could take you."

I shook my head, a smile playing on my lips. "I feel like something else is coming, and I don't like it."

Chase looked off into the distance, nodding tightly. "Our wolves are on edge. I know the Redwoods and Talons are doing what they can, but all of the attacks recently have been on our two lands."

I didn't know if it was intuition or just our wolves on edge.

"Why are you two just standing here?" Steele asked as the Enforcer came to our side, glaring.

"Just thinking of you. And how pretty you are." Steele rolled his eyes and tried to punch his Alpha. Then the two were rolling on the ground and snarling, and I sat back, wondering if I should start laying bets for when Steele got his ass handed to him. It would probably be soon.

"Anyway, when you two are done, we should probably get back to that m—" The wards pulsed again and we were knocked off our feet.

The first thing I did was roll back to my feet and search for my mates, my wolf ready to shift and fight.

Nico was already moving, Adalyn behind him.

"Chase, they're at the north gate. And they brought a fucking army," Cruz called out. Steele was already on his phone, shouting orders to his lieutenant to go to his warriors.

I pulled out my phone and called my Pack, needing to know they were safe.

"Our den's secure, as are the Talons and Redwoods. It's just here," I said as I slid my phone back into my pocket and ran alongside my mates towards the north gate.

"This ends today. I'm fucking tired of this," Chase growled.

"Damn straight. Never again."

I pressed a hard kiss to both of my mates' lips, as Chase did the same to Skye's, and then we moved forward, the front gate coming into view.

Trees were on fire, smoke billowing from them.

Hordes of vampires slid out from the trees, most of them with full cognitive power. They had been planning this for weeks, months, years.

This would not be our end. No, we would fight.

"Ronin is down!" Cruz said as he dragged the small wolf—still in wolf form—forward. Wren ran forward, put

269

her hands on his body, and nodded tightly. "He'll be fine. He doesn't need the antidote. He's just knocked out, a couple of broken ribs." She gave orders to her team, and Ronin was slid off to the side as we all pressed forward.

Over the din of power and magic stood Valac. He wore full leather warrior garb, not something for show as he normally did. He gave out orders to his own lieutenants and firsts, that wild manic panic in his gaze just the beginning. Even though he was still insane, he could plan this. And he was prepared.

Chase gave orders and I listened. My wolf didn't fight the orders and went to the quadrant we were assigned to. As the vampires came forward, our leagues of wolves, bears, cats, witches, and humans all came forward to meet them.

"I would rather you not be here," I whispered to Adalyn and she glared at me. "But I want you here at the same time. I just want you safe, so be the fierce kickass warrior princess that you are, and then I can fight with you later."

"You better be the damn perfect alpha, Alpha," she growled before she bit down on my chin, marking me slightly, and Nico grinned from her other side.

"You took the words out of my mouth. Be safe, and don't fucking get hurt."

And then the fight truly began. There was no more time for words, no time to plan.

Valac snarled. "Take the den down. Take the Central and Aspen Alphas. Take their mates. Take what is mine. This is only the beginning. We will take yours, and then we will take every den here. We will be the predators. The survivors."

Ten vampires came forward, some with blades, some with guns, most with just claws. I ducked the blade of the first one, jumped out of the way of the bullet of the next. Adalyn pushed down the vampire with the gun, snapped his neck, and dismantled the gun quickly. Though we could use them, and did use our own weapons, a weapon that the vampires used wouldn't be much help. We didn't know what kind of magic coated it, and we weren't about to get shot with our own guns.

Adalyn pulled out her blades and continued to provide a path to get through, slicing through the vampires' veins and arteries as if they were nothing. I looked over at Nico, his face covered in the blood of his enemy, and we both snarled, ready to protect our people.

A vampire came from behind Adalyn, and she whirled but Nico was there, slamming his foot into the ground, and a wall of dirt buried the vampire.

I blinked over at my mate, who shrugged. That new power was something we would have to talk about more later.

Valac was coming closer, cutting through the wolves nearest him. I was too far away to protect the smallest one, and when the wolf let out a whimper, hitting the ground with a lifeless thud, Chase roared, and he killed three vampires in one blow and kept moving.

Chase and Skye were together, the Alpha's mate, a fierce predator who helped make sure every single vampire that Chase hit was actually down for good.

On the other side of them, Dara held up her hands, dark fire blazing between each palm as she shot a swath of flames down the line. The enemy screamed, and she staggered, using far too much power protecting those around her. Cruz and Steele were on either side of her, taking down whoever came near her and protecting their den. But damn it, from the look on both men's faces, they didn't like Dara being out in the thick of it either. But there was no stopping that witch, not with the power she held.

Hayes, in his polar bear form—throwing aside his secrecy apparently—barreled through vampires right and left, using his dinner plate-sized paws to slice through vampires with one swipe. The world didn't know of cat or polar bear shifters as far as we knew, but with Hayes in bear form and Audrey having fought in cat form out in public before, the secret would be out if any satellites or drones were watching, and with this kind of attack, they *would* be watching.

Hayes roared, taking down another vampire in front of him with his giant paw. Disemboweled, the vampire screamed and hit the ground before Novah and Wynter came forward, using their swords, blades, and guns to take out anyone that polar bear didn't.

Audrey and Gavin were on the far side, having come back from patrol, their moves swift as if they had been fighting partners and mates for endless lives.

Another bomb went off, and we hit the ground before coming right back up, ignoring the black shard magic that came towards us, because Wren and her team were there, flinging out antidotes towards everybody that they could.

They weren't injectables but spells themselves, and she tossed them into the air, then down on the ground to create a wave of protection for us.

Valac's first in command, a vampire with red hair and redder eyes, came forward and pummeled Nico. He came out of nowhere, surprising all of us, and Nico hit the ground, a gash on his chest.

I roared and ripped the man's head off with one thrust. He tried to stab me even before it happened, but Adalyn came forward and sliced the man's arm off with her blade.

The vampire hit the ground, and we dropped next to Nico. Adalyn went to her hands and knees, covering Nico's wound with her palms. Blood gushed out between her fingers and she cursed.

When a trickle of blood slid out from between Nico's lips, my wolf shot to the forefront and I howled.

Because we did not have *our* Healer here. Wren wasn't our Healer. We just had medics, and I wasn't sure they would be enough.

I looked around in panic as Wren came forward, her eyes wide.

"I don't know. I don't know," she frantically muttered under her breath as she came forward, going down on her knees next to Adalyn. I hovered above them, protecting them as others tried to get to us, but nobody else could come near us to help. Everybody had their own grouping of vampires, and it was brutal. Wolves went down one by one, blood smeared the ground, the scent of smoke and death filling the air.

But something tugged on my mating bond and I looked over at Wren, who put her hands over Adalyn's, tears streaming down the Healer's face.

"I don't know. I think...how is it working?" Wren looked up at me, eyes wide. "I can feel him along my bonds. Not as Pack, but as something *different*."

Everything clicked then, hope beginning to bloom. "The alliance. We're blood bound."

She nodded, then looked down at Nico. "I could heal this." And then a wide smile covered her face. "I can *heal* this."

As healing energy warmed along the mating bond, Chase looked over at us from across the battlefield, eyes wide.

I knew instantly that this changed everything.

Because if our Healers could heal over Pack lines, it gave us a new boost, and we were closer as an alliance than ever.

When Wren finally finished and staggered back,

Chase was there, having cut through more of the enemy to hold her up.

"Did you use too much energy?"

She shook her head. "No, it's like I got a boost of energy from the others. I can feel the other Healers, just for an instant. At least I could. Wow. Okay. *I can do this*." She looked over at me, smiled wide, and then followed her team to help another fallen soldier, her body radiating with hope and energy.

I held out my hand and helped Nico up. He leaned against Adalyn for a minute, kissed the top of her head, and nodded tightly. "We can do this. I'm okay."

"Don't fucking do it again," I growled before crushing my mouth to his, turning at the exact moment I needed to, claws out.

Valac came forward far faster than I expected. He still had that dark witch and vampire magic that let him move faster than anything else on the battlefield.

I didn't think other vampires could do it, but I wasn't sure. It didn't matter, though, because it was Valac against us as the others fought their own battles. Chase had pulled back, protecting Wren as she moved from soldier to soldier, saving those she could.

But now it was my mates and me against Valac, and this would end.

As Adalyn touched the back of my arm and Nico touched my hip, something extraordinary happened.

Something I wasn't expecting.

The triad bond between us flared, intense heat that sizzled before it pushed out of my chest. Visible light slammed out of my mates and me, and I staggered, holding the other two up. Valac's eyes widened as the light hit him full force and he fell back. He tried to get up as quickly as he had before, but the light pushed him again and again and again.

When it stopped, Valac looked up at us and finally, *finally*, I saw the fear that I should have seen all this time.

The man, this monster, had killed our people, had terrorized us. He had used his power to take my mate and to hurt those that he thought weaker than him. He was the symbol of war that would come if the vampires truly ruled.

He was the man who threatened us all.

My wolf rose up, ready for power, for life. "This is the end. You don't get to do this again. Ever."

I didn't know how I knew, but I did. Our triad bond had been for a purpose. We had come together for a reason. Not only because we were mates but because we had *a purpose*. This triad bond could do something. It could flare and stop Valac from moving as fast to counteract his magic. If we could find a way to use this and our other bonds, we could change the game. We could protect our people. But for now, we had to stop this man.

"You might have gained something, wolf, but you will be nothing. My master's waiting. If I fall, there are countless more of us. People you don't even realize in your depths. You will lose everything. Just like I have."

"I'm done listening to you," Adalyn growled. "And you're done hurting my family."

Adalyn slid her blade into Valac's heart as I twisted his neck and Nico pulled the man's body, decapitating Valac with a blade to the heart, blood seeping into the ground.

And as their vampire general died on the battlefield, with broken promises and without a single scream, the other vampires tried to flee. But they were no longer under the command of their general. And our wolves were stronger.

In the end, some got away, but not many. We were able to defeat the enemy. I stood with blood on my hands and on most of my body and looked down at my mates, my eyes wide.

"How the hell did we make that triad bond work like that?" I asked.

Adalyn shook her head. "I have no idea, but we need to figure it out."

"Damn straight. Because what if other bonds, not triad, can do it? What if our mating bonds can counteract vampire magic?" Nico asked.

Others around us who had been listening nodded and started asking questions, but when Audrey came forward, Chase beside her, I looked around at the battlefield and knew that this conversation would have to wait.

"We've lost five," she whispered.

Chase let out a mournful howl, and I lowered my head in respect.

Audrey raised her chin, her eyes fierce. "They lost a lot more than us, and I don't know what else is out there. We're only just now doing the count." She let out a shuddering breath as Chase moved forward.

"Lily's missing. She was fighting alongside Wynter, but when a clutch of vampires came forward, they took her. I don't know what they want with her, but they have her."

Adalyn growled low, painful, and I held her close, knowing I needed to keep her safe. I needed to keep everybody safe.

"We stopped Valac," I said into the painful silence. "It might not be the end, but we killed the general. We stopped his magic. We have the antidote. This is something. We can't forget that. That we were Pack. All of us. Maybe of different Packs and different Alphas, but together we are power. And we cannot forget."

"Pack for all, Pack forever," Chase said.

As we threw our heads back and howled, I held my mates close and knew we had to take the victory for what it was. A first step, and hopefully closer to the final one.

But my mates were alive, I was alive. And in the end, that was what was important. And that was what I was going to think about until the end of my days.

CHAPTER
TWENTY-TWO

Adalyn

"I'M GLAD YOU'RE HERE," AUDREY SAID AS SHE hugged me close, then practically pushed me into my seat.

I rolled my eyes at her but settled into the couch as Dara handed me a cup of tea and Skye covered me with a blanket. Wren stared at me, then held out her hand.

I rolled my eyes, then placed my palm in hers. She hummed a bit, then smiled.

"The baby's doing okay. It's kind of nice that I can sense that. I think the moon goddess wants to ensure you have eyes on you at all times."

Cole snarled, "Considering she keeps trying to get herself blown up, I don't blame the moon goddess for allowing the other Healers to work across the bonds of Pack."

"I didn't purposely do it. Breathe, will you?"

He glared at me, placed a kiss on the top of my head, and then went to speak with Chase.

I shook my head and rolled my eyes.

We were at the Aspen den to go over what happened during the attack where Valac had died.

I could not believe the vampire was dead. That part of this was over. It didn't feel real that the person that had been trying to throw his vampires at us for so long was gone. That overwhelming sense of doom, though, hadn't escaped, and that worried me. Because if Valac was gone, who would step into his place?

We had chosen to meet at the Aspen den because this was where the focus of these attacks had been. Yes, each den had to deal with small incursions, but it was the Aspens under constant attack.

So while it wasn't my Pack any longer, it was still my home, just like all four dens were becoming one large Pack.

Each of the Alphas and their mates were here, and the hierarchy of the Aspens were here as well. It worried me to have so many dominants and leadership in one room, but we were in the center of the den, and the wards were strong right now. The witches that we had left were working hard to keep them so. Everybody was on high alert. But we had to plan this, and our wolves needed to be with others.

"How's the tea?" Nico asked.

I took a sip and hummed. "Perfect. I take it you're the one who made it for me?"

He grinned and pressed a kiss to my lips.

"Of course I did. I know what my mates like."

"Oh, be still my heart," Wren said as she fanned herself.

Nico flushed, kissed me again, then went off to talk with Hayes, the Omega of the Aspens, and my friend.

Steele and Cruz were growling with one another in a corner, and I knew that they would break it up soon and go speak with Cassius. While Cassius didn't have a title within the den, he was an upper-level soldier and lieutenant for the Enforcer.

We needed to make a battle plan for this next phase, and we needed to find Lily.

I rubbed my hand over my heart and Audrey gripped it and kissed my palm.

"We'll find her. She's alive. I have to believe it."

Chase met my gaze over Audrey's, his jaw tightening.

He didn't feel her. There was no bond anymore along the Alpha bonds of Pack. That didn't necessarily mean she was dead, as I knew none of them had felt her death. But in the craze of battle, they might have missed it. I just had to hope that somehow she had lost her bond to the Pack when she had been taken and we would find her. We needed to find my friend.

Kade, the Alpha of the Redwood Pack, cleared his throat. "I'm glad that we all could meet here today. That we're able to take a moment to go over what happened, to make some initial plans. But first, I'd like to say a few words."

His mate grinned at him. "Of course, you want to say a few words. You love speeches."

Nico cleared his throat. "Uncle Kade, you really do like speeches."

He narrowed his gaze at my mate and just shook his head. "What I wanted to say was our alliance is strong. We four Packs have been through hell, sometimes literally, together. We have faced the worst of humanity, the worst of what lies beneath that humanity. And we have persevered. We are strong together because we have this openness. Because we communicate with one another and try to find a balance between power and passion and peace."

"Say that three times fast," Gideon, the Talon Pack Alpha, mumbled under his breath. His submissive mate elbowed him in the ribs and we all laughed.

"What I'm trying to say is, while we are here as a war council, to go over everything that has happened, we are also here to welcome three people who are dear to our hearts."

I froze and looked around as everyone smiled.

"It's a full moon out there, you know," Chase added.

"This won't be a mating ceremony, but the moon goddess is bright tonight and beckons us. I think we need to go outside and listen."

"I thought I was supposed to be the one who proposed?" Cole asked as he laughed.

I handed Audrey my tea as I stood up. "Are you serious? A call to the moon goddess around the three of us during a war council?"

Nico shrugged. "I don't know. I kind of like the idea of ending this conversation about loss and death with a sign of hope."

Cole grinned, and that's how I found myself surrounded by three of the four Alphas of the alliances. I stood next to the fourth, holding his and Nico's hands, as they held each other. We stood in a circle, our friends of the Aspens and Centrals and the Alphas and their mates surrounding us.

This wasn't a mating ceremony. That would come later. Now, this was a promise, a call to the moon goddess herself.

I closed my eyes, lifting my head up to the moon goddess, and I heard her voice.

Something that had never happened to me before.

Something that I knew would never happen again.

"I'm sorry for changing your rules. For changing your path, dearest Adalyn."

I froze, and I wasn't sure anyone else could hear.

"This is just for you, because this is your moment.

These two were always yours. I'm sorry that fate broke what could have been. But this is your future. Your path. Your promise. I know that you will do great things with these men by your side. I know that you probably resent me for taking away that choice.

"But there needed to be three of you in that battle. And your child needed to be born at a certain time. You'll understand later. Your child will be safe. I promise you that. But for the war that is coming, they needed you. And I know you are so strong, my dearest Adalyn. The strength in your veins puts mine to shame and I am joyous for it.

"I didn't want you to be so strong that you didn't see the weakness you were allowed to have. For they are your weaknesses. Your pure and unadulterated hope.

"Love them, and know that they were always yours. And you would have chosen them. But I wanted to make sure you knew that you could. I love you, dearest Adalyn. For I am your goddess, but you are also mine. And while there is purpose to fate, there is also purpose to choice. So know that you would have chosen.

"They were always yours."

I opened my eyes and tears fell down my cheeks. I looked around as everybody stared, the women crying, Nico and Cole staring at me.

"Did you hear her?"

"She spoke to me, about choice, she called me her dearest Nico," Nico said with a laugh.

I looked around, and I understood.

"She spoke to all of us at once. I didn't know she could do that."

"She's the moon goddess. I think she could do anything," Cole said with a laugh. "At least with us."

"We were always supposed to be. And we always will be," Nico added. "This can be our engagement mating party. Our purpose. I love you."

"And I love you both."

"And I love you more," Cole growled, and I laughed as my mates held me close and our friends gathered.

We had followed the chaotic path of the goddess, but we were mates. We were everything.

I didn't need the white dress and the flowers and the long road of dating and wondering and hoping. I had what I wanted, even if I hadn't realized it at the time.

And as I looked at the four Alphas later, standing under the moonlight as their power radiated off in ways I couldn't even contemplate, I knew that all of these Alphas needed their mates. They needed their foundations.

The war wasn't over. It couldn't be.

Not with the demons still out there, not with Valac's master.

I had my mates and my child. I slid my hand over my stomach and smiled softly.

And I would fight for the future. Our future.

For we were Pack. All of us.

And we were survivors.

CHAPTER
TWENTY-THREE

Malphas

Malphas took off his jacket and hung it on the hook. With a sigh, he looked around his small home and knew it was only the waypoint between two parts of his life. This was the gentle professor's look, one that worked for the part he was playing. He smiled and went to the liquor cabinet to pour himself a finger of whiskey. Or maybe three.

It had been a long day, after all, and playing someone else was never easy. But then again, he was a demon. It's what he did best.

He turned at the sound of ice in the glass and smiled.

"You're here, darling."

His consort came forward, two glasses of whiskey in her hands.

"I know sometimes you like it neat, but on the rocks just sounds better. And the tinkling sound makes me happy." She grinned and handed over her glass.

He tipped his to hers before he drank it in one gulp. He didn't care about the taste at that moment. Just the fact it would help take off the edge for a bit.

"I see you're healing well."

His consort shrugged and set down her empty glass. "You have the best Healers, my love. But what would you have of me now?"

He slid his thumb over her lips and she opened her mouth. When she sucked on the tip, he groaned and went deeper. She gagged slightly and he smiled before sliding his thumb back out and licking her wetness. "You know what needs to be done." He slid his fang into his thumb, letting the blood well. He pushed his thumb back into her mouth and she shuddered, her body quaking from power. It was almost too much for her nearly human body, and he knew one day, if he went too hard, it would break her.

But he wanted to break her, as he had before. When she had been sweet and free. Of course, she'd never been in the light. She'd always been meant to be his. Always held that darkness that made her perfect for him. And the world would know exactly who stood at his side.

Until he was tired of her, but she didn't need to know that.

His consort licked her lips and ran her hands over her ample hips. "The more demon blood I have in me, the more I feel like I can do anything. This power, it's awakening me."

Malphas smiled again, leering. "Of course, consort. Without my power, you would be nothing. But we both know that."

She rolled her eyes and fluttered her fingers at him before going to pour him another drink.

Only his consort could disrespect him like that, but he knew later, when she felt the magic and power within, she would understand her place.

She was his—a demon's consort.

"I'm ready for the next step. To do what needs to be done."

"You've already done so much, consort." He stood behind her and wrapped her hair in his fist. He pulled it back and slid his hand up her shirt to cup her breast, and she moaned. Her nipple pebbled against his skin, and he licked his lips. "You know who you need to take out. Who you need to end. The power within her needs to be stopped."

Lily turned towards him, a sly smile on her face.

"Of course, we'll take out the witch. We took out the coven. We can do anything. You're my mate, my consort. My everything. I'll kill her just like I killed the others. And they'll never know what happened. They never knew me. But you did, Malphas. You always have."

He pushed her hair back from her face and crushed his mouth to hers, his cock hard against her stomach.

His consort would take out the witch and stop all those who came against them.

He might have lost the general, but he was only the first wave.

The vampires were his progeny, but they were not his finale.

She would be.

And the Aspens had no idea.

CHAPTER
TWENTY-FOUR

Dara

My back ached, but it didn't pulse or feel like someone was stabbing it with jagged knives, so I considered that a plus. See? I was getting better. Or at least I was believing my own delusions in which I considered I *could* be feeling better.

I rubbed my temple, my hands shaking, and I slowly let my palms press together in front of me. I closed my eyes and thought of the moon goddess.

"You might not be my goddess, you might be for the wolves, but I'm here. And I could really use your help."

Like always, there were no answers. The moon

goddess didn't speak to me. Because I wasn't a shifter, nor did I have elemental magic like the others thought I should.

I wiped the tears from my face, only just now realizing I had been crying. I didn't know if it was from the exhaustion or the pain.

I was just so tired of everything.

I loved my Pack. I loved the way that they surrounded me and did their best to help me. But I just wanted someone to understand. And it wasn't their fault that they didn't. It wasn't their fault that they couldn't. They literally couldn't understand my magic. As it was, I was afraid I didn't either.

I had stared into the abyss and seen what I had lost. What I could lose. I had seen the force of the magic within my veins, and I knew that if I touched it, if I went any further than I already had, it wouldn't only be my soul at risk.

It would be the soul of this Pack itself. And I refused to be its downfall. There were enough monsters in the darkness waiting to gut this Pack.

I would not be the reason we fell.

I was a harvester death witch. I literally held death in my hand. I would not be the balance of fate that let us fall into that darkness.

I just wished I could be a pretty earth witch. One who could make plants grow and use the soil to make power. I could push waves of dirt and roots and rock in order to fight my battles. Just like Nico was learning to do. He was learning to become a true earth witch. He would master it and he would be glorious and he would help this new coven, if they could actually build one.

And I was so afraid I would be on the outside looking in again. I wasn't who they needed me to be.

And with each wave of magic from the vampires against our den, I knew it wouldn't be enough.

I knew I would need the friends from my past, even if it might kill me.

I would have to reach out to her, to the others.

The coven had fallen. They had forsaken us.

And I knew the rest would come soon.

Someone knocked at the door and I stiffened.

I knew that knock. How could I know the way that somebody hit their knuckles against wood?

It made no sense. I wasn't a wolf, a cat, or a bear. I couldn't scent what was on the other side of the damn wood.

But here I was, hearing it. Knowing it was *him*.

The person that I couldn't face.

The person who hated me beyond all reason.

And frankly, I didn't blame him.

I rolled my shoulders back and made sure my hair was in its proper place. I had put it in a bun to make me look like a school marm ready to inflict torture against some child. It fit the persona I needed for the day.

The wacky witch with hair all in disarray wouldn't

work. Not when it felt like I had no control on the inside. I needed to look like I knew what I was doing on the outside.

I let out a breath and opened the door, meeting the gaze of the man who hated me.

He stood there, broad shoulders, strong nose and jaw. His eyes were gold, the wolf at the front. He needed a haircut, his hair starting to curl now with the humidity. His lips were full, his muscles just—he was gorgeous. The star of my wet dreams for far too long, even though I would never allow him to feel that. The fact that I had taken an herb to control my scent in the past so he wouldn't know what I felt around him only made me embarrassed.

"We need to talk."

I opened my mouth to tell him to go away, to tell him I didn't need to speak with him. It was a lie, but it was the only thing I could say. Yet he didn't give me the chance. He pushed past me, his shoulder running into mine. I still wore my heels, the heeled boots making me tall. He was still far taller.

"Sure, Cruz. Come on in. How are you doing this evening? I don't have any bread or tea for you, or even cookies. Maybe some biscuits? I don't know. What would a nice, homely woman want when they have a man over uninvited."

He growled at me, a low menacing growl that set me

on edge. My spine stiffened and the magic at my fingertips burned. I wanted to lash out.

But I couldn't. Not with him.

And once again, I hated myself.

"We need to talk," he snapped once more.

I closed the door behind him, grateful that the spell I had placed around my home kept it soundproof. It was hard enough to keep my secrets, to keep my privacy in a den full of shifters with enhanced hearing, taste, smell, and everything else. But it was harder when it was Cruz.

"And what do we need to talk about, fair Heir?" I asked, a teasing lilt to my voice.

He was the Heir of the Aspen Pack. The second in command. The one who would rule if something were to happen to our Alpha.

He held a mantle of strength and power.

And I had touched it once, that power.

And I never wanted to again. It wasn't that I couldn't handle it, because I knew I couldn't at all. No, it was because the demon within me, not a true demon, but the witch of darkness, wanted that power.

Craved it.

And I was not her.

"We need to talk about the fact that you're my mate, and you know it."

I staggered back, surprised he would even say that out loud. We did not speak of that. He did not speak of it.

"I don't know what you're talking about."

"Don't fucking lie. *Mate*."

"You're wrong. I'm not your mate."

He laughed, a mocking one that made me want to go to my knees and beg for forgiveness.

"You're my mate, but if you don't want to talk about that, fine. For now. Instead, we can talk about how you ruined my life."

I flinched, my hand going up to my face as if he had slapped me. "You don't mean that."

"You brought me back," he whispered, his voice barely above a murmur. He was in front of me then. I could feel the heat of him, scorching me from the inside out. "You brought me back," he repeated. "I want to know how."

"Cruz."

I couldn't speak of it. We both knew why. Or at least, I thought he knew. We needed to keep it buried. It was the only way to stay safe.

"I want to know why you did it. And I want to know why you're dying because of it and didn't tell me."

And with that, the wards around my soul shattered.

Next in the Aspen Pack series?

Find out what happens to Dara and Cole and the new Pack lore in Harbored in Silence!

WANT TO READ A SPECIAL **BONUS EPILOGUE** FEATURING COLE, NICO, AND ADALYN? **CLICK HERE!**

A NOTE FROM CARRIE ANN

Thank you so much for reading **Mated in Chaos!**

This book was a little different for me because I was able to play around in not one, but three Packs lol. The Central Pack has a long history in my heart and in this world, so being able to redeem them a bit was so satisfying! Showing them thriving and having a new world was exactly what I needed.

I always knew Cole was going to be in a poly romance, so I was grateful that I was able to write that into the Aspen Pack series.

Next up? We're heading to the world of magic and dark forces while the Aspen Pack cleans up the messes from the previous battle. I am having so much fun with this series and I hope you love Harbored in Silence when it releases next! Dara and Cruz have some explaining to do!

The Aspen Pack Series:

Book 1: Etched in Honor

Book 2: Hunted in Darkness

Book 3: Mated in Chaos

Book 4: Harbored in Silence

Book 5: Marked in Flames

And if you're in the mood for a paranormal romance outside the world of the Aspens:

The Ravenwood Coven Series:

Book 1: Dawn Unearthed

Book 2: Dusk Unveiled

Book 3: Evernight Unleashed

WANT TO READ A SPECIAL BONUS EPILOGUE FEATURING COLE, NICO, AND ADALYN? CLICK HERE!

If you want to make sure you know what's coming next from me, you can sign up for my newsletter at www. CarrieAnnRyan.com; follow me on twitter at @CarrieAnnRyan, or like my Facebook page. I also have a Facebook Fan Club where we have trivia, chats, and other goodies. You guys are the reason I get to do what I do and I thank you.

Make sure you're signed up for my MAILING LIST so you can know when the next releases are available as well as find giveaways and FREE READS.

Happy Reading!

ALSO FROM CARRIE ANN RYAN

The Montgomery Ink Legacy Series:

Book 1: Bittersweet Promises

Book 2: At First Meet

Book 2.5: Happily Ever Never

Book 3: Longtime Crush

Book 4: Best Friend Temptation

The Wilder Brothers Series:

Book 1: One Way Back to Me

Book 2: Always the One for Me

Book 3: The Path to You

Book 4: Coming Home for Us

Book 5: Stay Here With Me

The Aspen Pack Series:

Book 1: Etched in Honor

Book 2: Hunted in Darkness

Book 3: Mated in Chaos

Book 4: Harbored in Silence

Book 5: Marked in Flames

The Montgomery Ink: Fort Collins Series:

Book 1: Inked Persuasion

Book 2: Inked Obsession

Book 3: Inked Devotion

Book 3.5: Nothing But Ink

Book 4: Inked Craving

Book 5: Inked Temptation

The Montgomery Ink: Boulder Series:

Book 1: Wrapped in Ink

Book 2: Sated in Ink

Book 3: Embraced in Ink

Book 3: Moments in Ink

Book 4: Seduced in Ink

Book 4.5: Captured in Ink

Book 4.7: Inked Fantasy

Book 4.8: A Very Montgomery Christmas

Montgomery Ink: Colorado Springs

Book 1: Fallen Ink

Book 2: Restless Ink

Book 2.5: Ashes to Ink

Book 3: Jagged Ink

Book 3.5: Ink by Numbers

Montgomery Ink Denver:

Book 0.5: Ink Inspired

Book 0.6: Ink Reunited

Book 1: Delicate Ink

Book 1.5: Forever Ink

Book 2: Tempting Boundaries

Book 3: Harder than Words

Book 3.5: Finally Found You

Book 4: Written in Ink

Book 4.5: Hidden Ink

Book 5: Ink Enduring

Book 6: Ink Exposed

Book 6.5: Adoring Ink

Book 6.6: Love, Honor, & Ink

Book 7: Inked Expressions

Book 7.3: Dropout

Book 7.5: Executive Ink

Book 8: Inked Memories

Book 8.5: Inked Nights

Book 8.7: Second Chance Ink

Book 8.5: Montgomery Midnight Kisses

Bonus: Inked Kingdom

The On My Own Series:

Book 0.5: My First Glance

Book 1: My One Night

Book 2: My Rebound

Book 3: My Next Play

Book 4: My Bad Decisions

The Promise Me Series:

Book 1: Forever Only Once

Book 2: From That Moment

Book 3: Far From Destined

Book 4: From Our First

The Less Than Series:

Book 1: Breathless With Her

Book 2: Reckless With You

Book 3: Shameless With Him

The Fractured Connections Series:

Book 1: Breaking Without You

Book 2: Shouldn't Have You

Book 3: Falling With You

Book 4: Taken With You

The Whiskey and Lies Series:

Book 1: Whiskey Secrets

Book 2: Whiskey Reveals

Book 3: Whiskey Undone

The Gallagher Brothers Series:

Book 1: Love Restored

Book 2: Passion Restored

Book 3: Hope Restored

The Ravenwood Coven Series:

Book 1: Dawn Unearthed

Book 2: Dusk Unveiled

Book 3: Evernight Unleashed

The Talon Pack:

Book 1: Tattered Loyalties

Book 2: An Alpha's Choice

Book 3: Mated in Mist

Book 4: Wolf Betrayed

Book 5: Fractured Silence

Book 6: Destiny Disgraced

Book 7: Eternal Mourning

Book 8: Strength Enduring

Book 9: Forever Broken

Book 10: Mated in Darkness

Book 11: Fated in Winter

Redwood Pack Series:

Book 1: An Alpha's Path

Book 2: A Taste for a Mate

Book 3: Trinity Bound

Book 3.5: A Night Away

Book 4: Enforcer's Redemption

Book 4.5: Blurred Expectations

Book 4.7: Forgiveness

Book 5: Shattered Emotions

Book 6: Hidden Destiny

Book 6.5: A Beta's Haven

Book 7: Fighting Fate

Book 7.5: Loving the Omega

Book 7.7: The Hunted Heart

Book 8: Wicked Wolf

The Elements of Five Series:

Book 1: From Breath and Ruin

Book 2: From Flame and Ash

Book 3: From Spirit and Binding

Book 4: From Shadow and Silence

Dante's Circle Series:

Book 1: Dust of My Wings

Book 2: Her Warriors' Three Wishes

Book 3: An Unlucky Moon

Book 3.5: His Choice

Book 4: Tangled Innocence

Book 5: Fierce Enchantment

Book 6: An Immortal's Song

Book 7: Prowled Darkness

Book 8: Dante's Circle Reborn

Holiday, Montana Series:

Book 1: Charmed Spirits

Book 2: Santa's Executive

Book 3: Finding Abigail

Book 4: Her Lucky Love

Book 5: Dreams of Ivory

The Branded Pack Series:

(Written with Alexandra Ivy)

Book 1: Stolen and Forgiven

Book 2: Abandoned and Unseen

Book 3: Buried and Shadowed

ABOUT THE AUTHOR

Carrie Ann Ryan is the New York Times and USA Today bestselling author of contemporary, paranormal, and young adult romance. Her works include the Montgomery Ink, Redwood Pack, Fractured Connections, and Elements of Five series, which have sold over 3.0 million books worldwide. She started writing while in graduate school for her advanced degree in chemistry and hasn't stopped since. Carrie Ann has written over seventy-five novels and novellas with more in the works. When she's not losing herself in her emotional and action-packed worlds, she's reading as much as she can while wrangling her clowder of cats who have more followers than she does.

www.CarrieAnnRyan.com